RANGER
HEAT

CAITLYN LYNCH

RANGER HEAT

The stories in the book were originally published as three novellas comprising the *Ranger Heat* series, *First Submission, Second Surrender* and *Third Thrills*.

Other Works by The Author

DANA'S DUO

ELEVATOR ENCOUNTERS SERIES
1. ELLIE'S ENCOUNTER
2. JULIET'S ROMEO
3. THE BEST MAN FOR LEAH
   (INCLUDED IN THE JUST YOU AND ME
   BOX SET)

SUNFISH ISLAND RESORT SERIES
1. FINDING CORY
   (INCLUDED IN THE TROPICAL TRYST
   BOX SET)

2. THE RELUCTANT BILLIONAIRE
   (INCLUDED IN THE BILLIONAIRE EVER
   AFTER BOX SET)

SHENANIGANS PRESS ANTHOLOGIES
STOCKING STUFFERS
RED HOTS
SUMMER HEAT

HALLOWEEN ANTHOLOGY (upcoming)

CONTENTS

First Submission

"Hey baby, I'm back!"

Selina smiled, looking up from the pot she was stirring at the stove. "In here, Mark!"

Her boyfriend came in, smiling as he saw she was busy cooking dinner. "Mm, smells good." He didn't bother to come over and kiss her, and she quashed a tiny pang of resentment. He rarely did things like that these days. "When's it ready?"

"Twenty minutes," she shrugged, and he nodded.

"Okay, I'm gonna have a shower."

She nodded, watching him strip off his jacket as he headed into the bedroom. "Did you get the job?" she called after him.

"Nah. It was crap anyway." He popped his head back around the doorframe. "We're gettin' by okay on what you make."

Because I'm working two jobs while you haven't got one! she thought about shouting at him, but the door closed, and she bit her tongue.

Mark came out a few minutes later, headed into

their tiny spare room to switch on the computer, and Selina sighed. Figured she might as well sort out the washing and take it down to the laundry room after dinner, since she had a rare evening off. Mark might get another interview and he'd want his best jeans washed and ironed.

Heading into the bedroom, she scooped up the clothes he'd strewn casually around the floor as he undressed, sat down on the edge of the bed to check the pockets. Mark was hopeless at leaving things in them — her questing fingers found a folded sheet of paper, drew it out.

It looked as though it might be important, something printed on a high-quality paper, so she unfolded it, blinked as she saw the name of a high-class hotel at the top.

What the hell was Mark doing there?

Her eyes scanned down. It was a receipt. A receipt from the hotel bar. Two beers... *and three Cosmopolitans?*

"What are you doing?" She looked up to see Mark standing in the doorway, frowning down at her.

"Just sorting the washing. What's this?" She waved the paper at him, already knowing that there was no answer he could give that would sound in any way reasonable.

"Oh," he shrugged, his eyes darting around shiftily. "I stopped for a drink to unwind, after I found I didn't get the job."

The paper crumpled in Selina's fingers. "And who drank the three Cosmos?" Her voice was icy cold with rage and hurt.

"Don't be like that, babe," he attempted to placate her, and she jumped to her feet, throwing the crumpled receipt at his feet.

"Thirty dollars of the money *I worked to earn*, you spent buying drinks for *another woman*? Fuck you, Mark! Just — fuck you!" she ran past him, grabbed her purse and her keys off the kitchen bench. Racing down the stairs and out of the building, she shoved the key into the lock of her old van, glaring daggers at Mark's near-new Camry parked right next to it. The car *her wages* was paying off.

Fuck Mark. Fuck him.

Finally getting the van unlocked, she started it after only a couple of grumbles from the engine. Dashing away hot tears, she pressed her foot down on the gas.

Her phone rang in her bag. She ignored it, clenching her teeth, until it went to voicemail.

She ignored it the next three times it rang, too, before finally fishing it out of her purse, switching it off and throwing it under the passenger seat.

She drove without really thinking about it, no fixed destination in mind. It wasn't until the fuel warning light flashed on the van's dashboard that she really paid attention; looked at her surroundings.

"Huh," Selina said aloud.

She was in her old neighbourhood, where she'd lived BM (Before Mark). Neon lights on a corner ahead made her smile. The club.

It had been her favourite hangout ever since she got her first fake ID and had been able to lie convincingly enough to be let in. Loud music and cheap drinks had been all she'd wanted, back then.

"What the hell. For old times' sake." There might even be one or two old friends there. It wasn't until she'd had the thought, that she realised Mark had slowly cut her off from her old social circle, wanting to be the centre of her existence, the sole focus of her attention. "Fuck him," Selina growled to herself, pulling her van into the parking lot and shutting off the engine.

She didn't keep her whole wardrobe in the back, but there was enough to make do. A stretchy, glittery black dress she never wore because she and Mark never went out. Her black suede bootees with a little heel, perfect for dancing. A quick slick of lip gloss and some dramatic eyeshadow and she was done. She found her small clutch purse and shoved in her keys, lip gloss and the few dollars in cash she had with her; hesitated as she glanced towards the front seat. A quick check of her phone showed fifteen missed calls, all from Mark. Selina firmed her lips, switched the phone back off and threw it under the seat again.

It wasn't busy; there was only a short line outside the door. To her surprise, Selina recognised one of the bouncers, and his eyes widened as he saw her. He waved her to the front of the line immediately, high-fived her with a grin.

"Hey, Tobin!" she returned the smile happily.

"Ain't seen you around here in a while, girl."

"Ain't been around," she shrugged.

"Good to see you anyway. Go on in."

She tried to hand him the five-dollar entry fee, but he waved her off. "Beautiful girl like you, don't need no money here. Sure there'll be plenty of guys fightin' to buy you drinks inside."

Smiling and shaking her head, Selina said "Ah yes, but then they might expect something in return."

"If they don't take no for an answer, I'll convince 'em different." Tobin clenched one meaty fist and gave her a wink. Laughing, Selina passed him and entered the club.

Inside, it was just as she remembered; loud and faintly seedy, bright lights flashing over a seething mass of humanity on the dance floor. Overcome by a wave of nostalgia, Selina grinned and waded in.

She danced with abandon, ignoring men who tried to dance with her, joining in with groups of girls who smiled at her with welcoming feminine solidarity if the men persisted. After about half an hour, hot and thirsty, she decided to take a break. She visited the bathroom first, jostled elbows at the mirror to refresh her lip gloss before heading upstairs to the upper bar, where it would be a little quieter and less crowded, and she might actually see someone she knew.

She bought herself a beer first, a Corona with a lime wedge in the bottle's long neck; poked the lime in with her finger before taking a long swig, sighing with pleasure as the coolness washed over her parched throat. Leaning on the bar she looked around for a long moment, scanning faces, a little disappointed not to see anyone familiar. Too late, she thought that she should have texted her old friends, found out if any of them would like to meet up.

Oh well. With her phone in the van, that wasn't happening now. Selina shrugged mentally and walked towards the balcony railing. She knew there was a big air vent there; it would be nice to stand there for a few minutes and cool off as she looked down at the dancing crowd below.

There was even a vacant space at the railing, no one either side for a good couple of feet. Selina stood, drinking her beer, letting the cool air wash over her.

"Buy you a drink?" a deep voice said in her ear.

"No thank you, I already got one," she said politely, lifting her beer and glancing around. She took a tiny nervous step back when she saw the man she'd just instinctively rejected; he was huge, even bigger than her bouncer friend, and while not unattractive he was mean-looking, with a jagged white scar slashing from the corner of one eye to his chin and hard blue eyes.

"You sure?" the big guy pressed, moving closer, but then a hand landed on his shoulder.

"Lady said no, Jim."

Selina blinked as the big guy seemed to shrink into himself, nodded submissively and backed away, turning to look for easier prey. A minute later he approached two girls sitting on a couch, who looked at each other and giggled before nodding at him.

Looking back at her saviour, Selina found he was already leaning on the railing, looking away again. He was very attractive in profile, deep-set eyes and a strong chin, carefully groomed black hair. Not as tall as 'Jim', he still had to be around six foot and was powerfully built, compact muscle under his tight black T-shirt.

"Thanks," she said impulsively, lifting her beer in his direction.

Dark eyes flickered towards her, and he nodded. "You're welcome. Jim ain't good with rejection. Didn't want any trouble."

"He's a friend of yours?" Selina asked, glancing over to where Jim was now sitting between the two girls on the couch. They were both hanging on his shoulders, looking at him appreciatively. Well, as she'd thought, he wasn't unattractive. But Selina had looked in those flat blue eyes and seen a predator.

"He's on my team," was the response, making her look the black-haired man over again. He had a certain look to him, a straight-backed stance, and though he was heavily muscled somehow she didn't get the vibe that he spent a lot of time peacocking in front of a mirror at the gym with dumbbells in hand.

Military, was her conclusion eventually, and her first instinct was to sneer, Mark's attitude towards anything connected with the government a knee-jerk reaction. But then – it was *Mark* who was the jerk. Selina smiled instead. "Well. Thanks again."

He just nodded, looking away and down at the dance floor again. Interest piqued, Selina studied him further. Black cargo pants, black boots polished to a high shine. Thick muscles swelling the sleeves of his tight T-shirt, black stubble on his jaw. It was hard to tell in the light but she suspected his skin was olivine, he looked Italian. He looked like some old Sicilian Mafia Don's enforcer, actually, the suggestion of leashed violence ready to explode without warning in the very stillness of that powerfully muscled form.

"Gettin' a good look there?" he said without looking at her, and Selina found herself blushing.

"Sorry. Didn't mean to stare," she offered, and found herself pinned by eyes so dark they looked black as he turned his head and trained the full intensity of his gaze on her.

"I'm sure a pretty girl like you don't lack for male attention, but you're a little too young and innocent for me." She was a pretty little thing, he thought; at first glance he'd thought her barely old enough to get into the club, but a second told him she was probably a little older, maybe about twenty-five. Light brown hair with blonde streaks through it fell just past her shoulders, swishing as she gave her head an adorable little toss, her doelike brown eyes flashing at him. Her indignation was rather arousing, actually. He felt his cock harden with interest.

He was in his late thirties, maybe even his early forties, Selina reckoned, at least fifteen years her senior if not more. She still lifted her chin and glared at him indignantly. "I'm not innocent!" Innocence was lost early when you grew up in the foster system. She didn't regret it. At least it had been by her own choice, even if she was only fifteen at the time.

Finally, he turned to face her fully, stepped a little closer. Even though he wasn't as tall as Jim, he was more imposing, somehow, but Selina held her ground, lifted her chin. "Indeed," he said softly, his eyes raking her over swiftly. For a long moment they stood there facing each other silently, and then Selina smiled.

"I'm Selina, Selina Bancroft."

He hesitated a moment before switching his beer bottle to his left hand and holding out his right. "Brody Cullane."

She put her hand in his; it was warm and dry, his grip firm. "Can I buy you a drink?" Selina nodded towards the empty beer bottle in his free hand.

Brody grinned suddenly, the expression transforming his face from ruggedly handsome to utterly gorgeous as a dimple flashed in his chin and his black eyes danced with amusement. Selina couldn't help but stare.

"That's new. Mostly it's me offering to buy girls drinks."

"Eh," Selina shrugged. "I'm a modern girl."

"So I see. Come dance with me," he requested abruptly.

"Okay." She'd only half-drunk her beer, but she set it down on a vacant table, accepted his offered hand.

Brody danced well, light on his feet and with a great sense of rhythm. He seemed to project a kind of aura as well, nobody even on the crowded dance floor bumped him or even invaded his space. Selina wasn't so lucky; someone cannoned into her after just a few minutes and she lurched forward – into the solid wall of Brody's chest.

Thickly muscled arms closed around her, and she looked up to find him glaring daggers at the hapless drunk who'd bumped her. Smoothly, Brody guided her off the floor, leading her around behind the main bar where it was a little quieter and they could hear each other speak.

"You alright?" he checked.

"Fine, it was just a bump," Selina shook her head, smiling.

"Idiot shoulda looked where he was going." One powerful arm remained around her, and the other came to rest on the wall beside her head now, pinning her in place. Selina wasn't objecting in the slightest. She smiled up at him and licked her lips, lowering her eyelashes seductively.

Brody's chest heaved with a quick indrawn breath, and then he bent his head, mouth seeking and hot over hers in a demanding kiss, his tongue thrusting between her lips instantly.

Certainly not innocent, still Selina had never been kissed like *that*, as though he wanted to devour her. *Conquer* her. Her hands came up to land on his ribs, twist her fingers in his tight shirt, and Brody growled in his throat, tongue thrusting into her mouth in a rough mimicry of sex.

Arousal had never hit her so hard and so fast. Selina whined into Brody's mouth, and suddenly his hand was behind her knee, lifting it against his hip, his groin grinding against hers as his hard body pushed hers hard up against the wall. She was wet instantly, soaking through the thin fabric of her panties. His elbow hooked under her knee, calloused fingertips gliding along under her thigh, pressing suddenly and firmly over her core.

A low rumble sounded deep in Brody's core as he felt how wet her panties were, and suddenly he was pulling her away from the wall, opening a door she hadn't even noticed, and dragging her inside. Some kind of storeroom, Selina vaguely noticed, crates and boxes stacked around, before the door was closed and she was shoved up against it, Brody's hungry mouth descending on hers again. She panted with need, her hands clawing at his shirt, desperate to feel some skin. She managed to drag it up, put her hands on his back, felt smooth skin shifting over hard muscle.

"Fucking *hot*," Brody rasped against her neck, dipping his head to suck on her throat, and Selina really didn't give a fuck that he'd be leaving a hickey there.

"Please," was all she could manage, and he laughed huskily, his stubble rough on her sensitive neck.

"Don't worry, beautiful, gonna give it to ya." His hand was lifting her knee again and she moaned, hooking her leg around his waist eagerly as strong fingers groped at her panties. She squealed a moment later as he ripped them away with a sharp twist of his wrist.

"Shut the fuck up, you're fucking loving it," he muttered roughly, and Selina couldn't even make herself gasp a denial, because it was so utterly, undeniably true. Two thick fingers plunged deep inside her pussy suddenly and she cried out ecstatically. His callused thumb rubbed hard over her clit and her hands clutched at his muscled arms as she shuddered.

"Uhhh," she moaned.

"Say my name. Brody. Say it."

"B-Brody," she panted as his fingers pumped hard. "*Please*."

"Good girl, you *are* a good little girl, aren't you?" He licked and sucked at her neck, his free hand tugging down the neck of her dress, pushing down her bra cup, wrapping around her breast and squeezing.

She'd never even imagined anything like this. Not

even when she and Mark had a make-up-after-a-fight fuck was it *anything* like this rough and dirty and *amazingly good*. The orgasm hit like a tidal wave and Selina's whole body shuddered, juices slicking Brody's hand to the wrist.

"Mm," he withdrew his hand, licked at his fingers, eyed Selina as she slumped back against the wall. "Lovely. Over here, beautiful."

She was almost boneless as he moved her, leading her over to a low table in the corner of the storeroom, bending her over it and pushing her skirt up her thighs. Unbearably excited at the thought of what was about to happen, she twisted her head to peer back at him, watching as he unfastened his pants and took his cock out. Swollen with arousal, flushed red, it was thick and hard. Selina moaned wantonly, spreading her knees apart. Wanting Brody to fuck her.

Pulling his wallet from his pocket he found a condom and rolled it on, stroking his cock as he gazed at her slender legs and rounded bottom, at the shiny trails of slick on her inner thighs.

"You're fuckin' gorgeous," he muttered hoarsely. "Gonna fuck you senseless."

Selina could only whimper and clutch at the far edge of the table as he rubbed the sheathed tip of his cock tauntingly over her, stroking it from her clit up to her hole and back down again, wetting it with her juices.

"Please," she sobbed, "Brody, please!"

"Good girl, you remembered I like it when you say my name," he praised, and pushed just the tip of his cock inside her.

She tried to writhe back against him, take him deeper, but a firm hand on the small of her back held her still against the edge of the table.

"No you don't, I'm settin' the pace here, beautiful," he dealt a small slap to her bottom. Startled, she let out a little squeak and stilled.

"That's it," Brody husked, letting the hand that had smacked her caress lightly over her buttock. "Easy now. No rush." Slowly, he pushed into her. It seemed to take forever, he was bigger than she was used to, longer and thicker; and by the time his groin was pressing against her ass she was yelping and panting frantically.

"Such a sweet tight little pussy," Brody's breath was hot at the back of her neck as he bent over her, and then he straightened up, gathering her hair in one hand, the other one grasping firmly onto her hip to hold her in place for him as he fucked her.

There was no lock on the door, someone could have walked in at any moment and found them, and somehow that made it even more titillating as Brody began to pump inside her, balls-deep one moment and almost completely withdrawing the next before slamming back hard to full depth. His hand in her hair pulled slowly, a remorseless tug that kept her back arched and her head up, and that little pain added to the pleasure she was already feeling drove Selina wild. Her nails scored at the tabletop, hoarse cries spilling from her lips as his rough thrusts jarred her whole body.

"Good girl," Brody said, looking down at Selina, writhing under his impalement. She was loving this, it was very obvious, and he marvelled at his good fortune. What were the odds of his finding a beautiful young thing in a club he'd only visited to keep an eye on his men? Willing and a perfect sub – God, what he wanted to do to her... he hardened still further at the thought, feeling his balls filling and tightening, a tingle up his spine warning his climax wasn't far off.

Determined that Selina was going to come again

too, he shifted his angle slightly, seeking her G-spot with his thrusts, rewarded as she suddenly stiffened, her moans becoming throatier and more desperate.

"That's it," Brody snarled, and he took his hand off her hip and slapped her outer thigh sharply as he thrust back in the next time. Tight muscles convulsed around him, and he grinned wickedly. "Like that, do you, beautiful?" He did it again, a little harder, and Selina came with a helpless wail, shuddering and clawing at the tabletop as ecstasy smashed her senses away.

A few more harsh thrusts and Brody was coming too, stilling and groaning deep in his chest, his hips pinning her down to the tabletop as his cock pulsed deep inside her still-clenching core, spurts of hot seed jetting up his cock in an apparently endless stream.

Slowly, his grip on her hair eased, letting her head down, and Selina put her forehead on the table and took deep, shuddering breaths. She felt him pull out, heard the wet slurp of the condom being removed, the hiss of his zipper.

"Hey," Brody reached out, smoothed Selina's dress back down gently, pulled her up to stand up and turned her round. The top of her dress was still displaced and he fixed it for her, put a finger under her chin and tipped her face up. "You alright, Selina?"

She looked a little shocky, her pupils dilated, and he wondered suddenly if she'd actually gone into subspace. The very thought made him start to feel aroused again, and he pulled her close, making her lean her head against his chest, cuddling her tenderly, humming soothingly under his breath, smoothing her messed-up hair. She'd been amazing, she deserved looking after, deserved more from him than a quick fuck in a club's back room.

Brody realised that he wanted that more. Wanted to

take his time with Selina, see what she was really capable of. Just thinking about seeing her on her knees for him, those big doelike eyes wide, was almost enough to get him hard again instantly.

"I ain't finished with you yet, beautiful," he said softly when he finally felt her relax against him. "We're staying in a hotel just on the next block. Will you come there with me?"

She nodded against his chest.

"Is there anyone you need to let know?"

A shake of her head, and then she looked up at him, biting her lip. "I probably shouldn't have told you that. Please don't be a serial killer?"

He chuckled quietly. "I promise I'll let you go alive."

"Oh good."

His hand was gentle as he smoothed her tangled hair, and then he slipped his phone from the thigh pocket of his cargo pants, tapped in a quick text message as they walked to the door, letting his team know he was heading back to the hotel.

Brody didn't look around as they left the club, just confidently leading Selina out, her hand held securely in his.

"Hey, Selina, off so soon?" Tobin said amiably as she walked out, giving Brody side-eye.

"Yeah, catch ya next time!" Selina deliberately made her voice bright and cheery, offering her hand for a high-five, knowing Tobin wouldn't hesitate to try and stop them if he suspected Selina might have been roofied. And while she knew the big bouncer could handle himself, some deep instinct warned her that he – and his colleagues – would be utterly outmatched against Brody, even if Jim and Brody's other friends didn't get involved.

Tobin high-fived her with a nod and a smile before

returning his attention to the waiting line. Brody slipped his arm around Selina's waist and drew her in close. She debated for a moment going to her van to get her phone – but no, fuck it, there'd just be a bunch more missed calls from Mark, and she really didn't want to think about him right now.

There was a 7-11 on the corner, and Brody led Selina in with a murmur of "Need more condoms!" that made her grin. Remembering she hadn't ended up having any dinner — she spared a moment to vindictively hope it had burned and Mark choked on it — she paused in front of the donut case.

"Hungry?" Brody came up behind her, basket swinging from his fingers, several bottles of neon-coloured energy drinks in it. His arm slid around her waist again, his face pressing into her neck, stubble lightly rasping her skin. "When did you last eat?"

"I had some leftover fried rice for lunch," she admitted sheepishly, and he sighed and shook his head.

"You're gonna need more energy than that, beautiful." His voice was a low, dark promise that made Selina shiver against him. "Get a donut, and they've got wraps and sandwiches too, pick one..." he walked away again, collected some trail bars and chocolate, and came back. Selina had picked a salad wrap and a donut, and Brody took them from her and carried them to the register. The bored cashier rang up the purchases and bagged them, and a minute later they were on their way again, the bag swinging from Brody's free hand.

The hotel had apparently had a renovation since Selina moved out of the area; it looked quite upscale now. Brody had a large room on one of the higher floors; she moved to the window and looked out over the bright city lights as he put the *Do Not Disturb* sign out and closed the door behind them.

"Second thoughts?" his voice was low behind her.

"No." She turned back around, looked up at him with clear eyes.

"Good. But I ain't touching you again until you've eaten, so have a seat." He pointed at the small table, the straight-backed chair beside it.

Selina sat down obediently and he put the salad wrap and a bottle of something blue in front of her. She raised her eyebrows at it.

"Electrolytes," Brody said succinctly, "you're gonna need them." He cracked a bottle of something green for himself, took a long swig. "I'm gonna take a shower. If you're gonna make a run for it, that's your opportunity."

She never even considered it. Just sat and ate her wrap, drank the blue stuff – which wasn't as disgusting as it looked – while he was in the bathroom. She'd finished and was sitting back, quietly sipping the last of the drink, when he came out, a towel wrapped around his waist, and Selina dropped the bottle. Fortunately there were only a few drops left in it and none spilled out.

"Holy shit!"

In his tight T-shirt, it had been pretty obvious that Brody was well-built. Now she saw the truth of it, and her eyes opened wide, because he was just *perfect*. Not the artificiality of a body-builder, but the sheer power of a man who'd earned his muscles through hard work and sweat. Broad shoulders and thick arms, a heavily muscled chest lightly furred with dark hair tapering to a thin trail down the centre of a perfect six-pack. She couldn't help but stare as her eyes followed that happy trail downwards, before he said her name and she jerked her head up to look him in the eyes.

He smirked down at her, and she totally failed to

resist the urge to lick off a droplet of water trickling slowly down the cleft between his thick pectoral muscles, past the dog tags that told her she was right, he was definitely military. Brody sighed as her tongue trailed over his skin, and then his hand knotted in her hair, pulling her lips away from his skin.

"Did I give you permission to do that?"

Selina blinked, her brows drawing down in confusion.

Brody tilted his head curiously, letting go of her hair. "Do you even know?"

"Know what?" she asked, puzzled.

"Selina..." he hesitated. "I thought you were a sub. A submissive. I'm a Dom – I thought – *fuck*."

Selina flushed. "I don't – I haven't ever..."

He was watching her closely. "Does the idea excite you?"

Mutely, she gave a tiny nod, her eyelashes sweeping down.

"You already trusted me with a great deal. You let me be rough with you back at the club, and I *know* you enjoyed it." Gently, he put his fingertips under her chin, made her look up at him. "Trust me again, Selina. Let me show you what you are. You were born for this."

She chewed on her lip silently, uncertain.

Brody sighed. "Why are you here?"

"Wh-what?"

"You're running from something. Trying to forget something. What is it?"

Goddamn, he's perceptive, Selina thought, a little stunned. "My boyfriend," she confessed. "I think – he cheated on me. Or tried to."

Brody nodded slowly. "Yeah, I bet he did." Then, when she looked offended, he sighed, moved to sit in the chair, and pulled gently on Selina's hand until she sat, a little nervously, in his lap. "Look, I could give you the standard platitudes, that he'd be stupid to cheat on a girl as beautiful as you, blah blah blah. That's what everyone else will say and it still won't make any sense. You want my theory?"

Curious now, Selina shrugged. "Sure."

"You're a born sub, and you don't even know. Which means that he isn't Dom enough for you. He might be bossy and a bit of an ass – yeah, thought so," when Selina's eyes widened. "But he ain't a Dom. Which means that you aren't getting what you *need*. And that means you aren't truly satisfied, and if in any relationship one partner isn't truly satisfied, the other one won't be either. *That's* why he's looking outside for satisfaction."

Selina sat very still, her thoughts whirling. Brody nuzzled lightly at her shoulder. "You know I'm right, don't you?" he said softly, his voice a low, growling rasp. "It's why you're here. Why you let me fuck you. It wasn't *about* getting your own back for his cheating. You knew the moment you looked at me that I could give you what you need. The way *he* never has. The way *no-one* ever has, unless I miss my guess."

Her cheeks slowly reddened, and she nodded. "Maybe – maybe you're right." He was certainly correct that she'd taken one look at him and not been able to look away.

He smiled, bit at her shoulder gently. "I'm not so Dom as to insist that I'm *always* right. But – yeah. I'm right."

That made her giggle, and he put his arm around her waist to hold her more firmly. "So – what happens if I trust you, then?" Selina flicked her eyes sideways to meet his, shy but unafraid. "I mean, I've read *Fifty Shades...*"

"Oh shit, forget all that. That guy's a creep and a fucking terrible Dom, gives us *real* Doms a bad name," Brody shook his head.

That made Selina grin. "He did seem rather... *contradictory.*"

"And not overly concerned with consent, either. About the only thing he got right was the safeword, even if he failed to respect it." Brody kissed her shoulder again. "So let's start there, hmm? You okay with the traffic light system? Green for go, yellow for slow down, red for stop?"

"Yes," Selina nodded in agreement.

"I don't have time to do much. I wish I did, wish I'd got time to explore everything with you, to show you what you're capable of, but I have to leave in the morning."

Unreasonably disappointed, she was about to ask why, but... *Military*, she thought, looking again at his dog tags. He couldn't tell her, even if he wanted to, she suspected, so she just nodded. "Okay."

"I'd need more equipment, too – it doesn't matter. We don't have it, so we'll start with the small stuff, yeah?"

"Sounds good," Selina agreed with a relieved little smile.

"All right." He nudged at her gently. "The first thing you'll learn is that you *must* obey when I use my Dom voice, okay? You'll know when I do."

"Okay," she said uncertainly, and then she jumped as his voice did indeed change, becoming flatter and harder, lower-pitched, almost a snarl.

"Get up."

Selina shot to her feet instinctively, earning an approving smile from Brody.

"Good girl. Now turn around and take your boots

off. Slowly. Give me a show."

She understood what he meant. Considering she had no panties – God only knew where they'd ended up when he ripped them off earlier – her skirt would ride up a long way when she bent down. Turning around, she bent at the waist, keeping her knees straight, and bent slowly, glancing at him between her legs.

"That's it," Brody murmured encouragingly, watching as Selina unzipped her boots, removed them both slowly. It was summer and her long slender legs were bare, tanned. "Hitch your skirt up for me as you come up."

She did it slowly, pulling the tight fabric up, stopping as she felt the hem touch her buttocks.

"Shuffle forward and put your hands on the bed."

Obeying, she flinched in sudden horror as she heard the click of a camera phone. "No! Red!"

"Okay." He lowered the phone, held it out to her. "Come here and look. Your face isn't visible. Your own mother wouldn't know you. But delete it, if you want. I just wanted something to remember you by."

She hesitated, looking at the image, her finger poised over the *Delete* icon. It was incredibly revealing, pornographic – but he was absolutely correct that she wasn't recognisable. Finally she handed the phone back. "No. You can keep it. But please don't share it, and please don't take any more?"

"Of course." He put the phone on the table, sliding it away. "I'm not going to do anything you don't want, beautiful," Brody said softly as she looked at it warily. "This is about trust, remember?"

"I remember." Uncertain what to do next, she stood still and waited.

Brody watched her for a moment, before nodding. "Okay. Good job using the safe word. Don't forget it, now. I'm not going to do anything without your full and enthusiastic consent, all right? I'm sorry I didn't think to ask your permission before taking a picture. I promise I won't take any more."

Selina nodded, relaxing a little more.

"Now," Brody dropped back into his Dom voice, "on your knees."

She would have obeyed that voice even if he hadn't commanded her to; something deep within her *recognised* it. Her knees hit the carpet almost before her brain processed the command.

"Do you like sucking cock, Selina?" his voice was soft again.

She thought about lying; in the end shrugged. "It's okay. I don't mind."

"What did I just say about *enthusiastic* consent?" He shook his head at her. "Your bossy idiot of a boyfriend just shoves it down your throat, doesn't he?"

She hung her head, wondering how the *hell* he could read her so well. "I don't like it in my throat," Selina admitted, barely audibly. "I can't breathe and I don't like that."

"Okay." He unfolded the towel at his waist, spread it back, parted his knees. "Why don't you show me what you *do* like to do?"

Her eyes widened as she got her first look at his cock. No wonder she'd felt full back in the club; he was *big*, thick and long, neatly cut; rising from a nest of crisp black curls he was only half hard right now but still sizeable.

He was beautiful, and Selina felt her mouth start to water. Swallowing, she moved forward on her knees, kneeling between his feet. Reached her hand out tentatively.

"Just your mouth," Brody said in his Dom voice,

"put your hands behind your back." More softly, he said "See if you can get me hard with just your mouth. Just the way you like to do it."

She nodded, looking up at him trustingly from wide doelike eyes, and Brody smiled wryly. "Looking at me like that you probably don't even *need* your mouth, beautiful."

Selina smiled shyly, turned her head to nuzzle against his muscled thigh. Held his gaze as she flicked her tongue lightly against his skin, tasting him. He tasted fresh and clean, hot water and soap, a faint masculine tang under that. Slowly she trailed her tongue in patterns up his thigh until she was nuzzling at his balls, flicking her tongue in delicate little swipes, before dragging it in one long lick right up the length of his shaft, swirling it around the tip.

"Mm," Brody's hand slid into her hair, and Selina tensed instinctively. Mark always held onto her hair when he wanted to fuck her throat – but Brody wasn't holding on, was stroking her hair, petting her like a cat, his breathing slow and easy. After a moment she began again, caressing his cock with her lips and tongue, mouthing the tip briefly before working back down again.

"Good girl," Brody said, and Selina realised he was indeed fully hard again. Pleased, she wrapped her lips around his tip, tongued the frenulum quickly as she bobbed her head in short little strokes. She could feel herself getting wet between her thighs too, shifted a little uncomfortably. She'd be dripping on the carpet in a minute.

"Oh, good, you're gooood," Brody sighed, still stroking her hair. "Mmmm. Lovely. All right, stop, beautiful."

Teasingly, she sucked a little harder, her cheeks

hollowing, tongue working quickly under the fat tip of his swollen shaft.

"I said *stop*." It was the Dom voice, and Selina froze, hastily pulling off.

"I'm sorry..."

"Sshh," he caressed her hair again, curved his hand under her chin and lifted her face, making her look at him. "I'm not gonna be harsh with you, since it's your first time as a sub. When you get your own Dom, you'll understand; you won't *want* to disobey, whether they use a Dom voice or not."

"I don't want to disobey *you*," Selina admitted. "I just want to please you."

He smiled, getting to his feet, towering over her where she still knelt on the floor. "Excellent," he purred. "I'm happy to hear that. Up you get, then, and take your dress off for me."

She stood at once, caught the hem of her dress and peeled it upwards, bringing the stretchy material up over her body and tugging it off over her head, leaving herself wearing only her bra.

Brody licked his lips. "That too," he said quietly, smiled as Selina immediately unclipped and removed the bra. "Very nice." He prowled around her slowly, surveying her. "Very, very nice." He trailed a finger up her spine from the cleft of her buttocks to the nape of her neck, his smile widening as she shuddered slightly, goosebumps springing up in the wake of his touch.

Leaning in behind her, he kissed her neck just below her ear, caught her earlobe in his teeth for a little nip. "Ever had your bottom spanked before, little girl?" He patted one rounded buttock lightly.

"N-no." She let out a little squeal of shock as she was suddenly grabbed around the waist by a powerful arm, yanked off her feet and placed across his lap as he sat back down on the chair and positioned her ass-upward, both hands held at the small of her back in one of his, her head hanging down towards the floor.

"Give me a colour, Selina." His free hand smoothed over her bottom.

It took a moment for her to realise what he meant. "Green," she panted.

"Good; you remember that. Tell me if at any point it becomes not green, all right?"

"Y-yes."

"Slow your breathing. Steady. You won't get the endorphin release if you don't relax into it." His voice was low and soothing, his hand gentle as he swept his hand in long soothing strokes from her lower back down to her upper thighs, and Selina found her breathing slowing in response to his order. *In. Out. In. Out.* She concentrated on slow, deep breaths, and was relaxing into an almost meditative state when the first strike landed on her right ass cheek. Her breath hitched in a gasp.

Brody's hand resumed the slow, soothing strokes. "Colour."

"Green." It was *more* than all right. The pain had seemed to radiate through her, transmuting to heat and arousal somewhere along the way. Her nipples were aching, her pussy leaking. "More. Please."

Her answer was a low, husky laugh, and then he struck again, a little lower. The spanks were firm but not hard; it was obvious to Selina that he wasn't using all his strength by any means, but the flat of his hand stung and she was sure her bottom would be red. She couldn't bring herself to care.

"What a good little girl," Brody murmured, after he'd delivered ten smacks. He admired the red marks, livid on her pale skin. "But what a *dirty* little girl. I can feel you, you know. Leaking on my leg."

Selina squeezed her eyes shut, embarrassed.

"Smell you, too. You smell *delicious*." Her thighs were a little apart, forced there by the way he was holding her, and his hand slipped between them, fingers stroking slowly, and she could hear the wet sound they made. His forefinger circled over her clit, and she moaned helplessly, but then he took it away and she heard him licking at it, tasting the juices he'd gathered. "You do taste good. Yes, I think I'll feast here tonight."

Brody's voice was low and dark, a threat and a promise in the statement making Selina shudder again. And then he scooped her up like a rag doll and tossed her onto the bed. She landed on her back with a shocked squeak, but he was after her in an instant, pushing her legs apart and lifting her hips, pushing two pillows under them to lift her ass up in the air.

"Bend your knees, put your feet on the mattress," he ordered, "yes, that's right."

She was spread wide open, completely exposed. Brody knelt on the end of the bed, looking down at her. "Play with your boobs," he ordered, "pinch those nipples, get them nice and hard. Pity I ain't got any clamps for you."

Selina had always enjoyed rough play with her sensitive nipples, but she'd never even *thought* of clamps. Her lips parted on a gasp as she pinched at the sensitive nubs, her eyes locked with Brody's as he watched her.

"Good," he purred, and then keeping his eyes on hers, he leaned down and licked a long, slow stripe from her opening to her clit, before pressing both his thumbs lightly on her clit, rolling the hood back, making his tongue into a point and teasing over it.

Selina bit down, hard, on her lip to try and make herself be quiet. Mark always told her she was too noisy (*your moaning's fucking distracting, like a fucking tennis player,* he'd say) but Brody lifted his head. "Don't do that," he said thickly. "Lemme hear you. I want to hear you come apart."

She hesitated, but he was staring at her, so after a moment she unclenched her jaw, let her lips part – and he licked her clit again. Her legs trembled as he kept going, soft breathy moans she barely recognized as her own escaping her mouth, rising in pitch to needy whimpers whenever he drifted away from where she *needed* his mouth to be. She felt him grin against her for a moment before he moved back up a little and *sucked* on her clit, hard. Selina arched off the bed with a wail that caught in her throat, gripping the sheets to keep from covering her mouth.

Brody didn't stop, kept going even after she'd arched and shrieked her way through a climax, kept working her clit even though she was at a fever pitch of sensitivity. It hurt, a little bit, and twice he stopped briefly and asked her for a colour.

Selina never considered saying anything but "Green. Oh God, yes, it's green, *please...*"

"You beg real pretty," he muttered gruffly before burying his face in her again. This time, though, as his teeth grazed her clit, his tongue and fingers stroked up between her labia before two thick fingers thrust sharply inside her.

Selina's knees shook. She was still playing with her breasts, tugging hard on her nipples now, roughly squeezing them in her fingertips. Brody made a pleased rumbling sound against her, pulled off for a moment to look down at her, spread out and vulnerable.

"So fucking pretty," he murmured, and dealt a

sharp little slap to her clit.

Selina screamed, jack-knifing upright, her head falling back with ecstasy. "More!" she begged frantically, and he laughed huskily and did it again.

"Oh oh *ohhhhhhhh*!" Selina's scream was extremely loud as she convulsed, the orgasm massive as it exploded through her, leaving her shaking and panting for breath.

Brody laughed quietly, reaching for a condom. "You *are* a noisy little thing. I like it."

She could barely function, certainly not resist when he moved off the bed and pulled her to the edge of it, turning her over, placing a pillow under her hips. "Want a good fucking, little girl?" his voice was low in her ear as he bent over her. "I think you do."

"Please," Selina whimpered as she felt his cock pushing at her.

"Real wet, aren't you? You liked that. You like being a dirty little girl for teacher, hey?"

"Yes, sir," she gasped out as he plunged in, fast and hard. "Oh God, sir, yes, please, teach me a lesson..."

"Gonna teach you a lesson all right, little girl. Gonna teach you what happens to naughty little girls who pick up bored soldiers in nightclubs." He wasn't even breathing hard as he fucked roughly into her, Selina's fingers clawing at the sheets. Strong hands clamped on her hips eliminated any possibility of her getting away, not that she wanted to; it felt too good, the drag and glide of his thrusts rubbing over exquisitely sensitive flesh.

One muscled forearm curled under her then, supporting her and holding her steady while he continued to pump, the other slid down her spine and in between them... Selina cried out in shock as a thick finger probed at her ass.

"You're gonna like this," Brody grunted, finally sounding a little breathless himself. "Gonna like this a lot, naughty girl. Only a pity I haven't got a dildo or something else to fuck you with while I take your ass. Have to make do with this, do you like this?"

She couldn't answer, lost for words, screaming incoherently into the mattress as his finger pressed deeper. She heard his dry, husky laugh again, and then there was a *second* finger and she lost contact with reality entirely.

Brody groaned as Selina tightened around him, felt a gush of wetness around his achingly sensitive cock. He'd been sternly holding himself in check but no longer saw any need as her body went completely limp under him, so he allowed himself free rein. A few swift, rough strokes later and he was coming too, his vision darkening briefly as he pumped himself dry in the little sub's body.

What a gorgeous little thing she was, he thought, pulling out finally, stroking her back. She'd blacked out, he suspected, took the time to gently arrange her in bed before going to dispose of the condom and checking his watch. Three-thirty. He and his team were moving on out at six. Oh well, a couple of hours' sleep was better than none at all, especially with his body still humming with satisfaction.

Setting his watch for a five-thirty alarm, Brody quietly moved around the room picking things up and tidying them before slipping into bed beside Selina. She curled towards him, putting her head on his chest with a small sigh, and he stiffened.

Oh well, no harm in it for one night, he thought finally. And she was a sweet little thing. He certainly hadn't expected to get *this* lucky. Shame they were heading back to base after recently completing training exercises nearby and he wouldn't see her again. Some other lucky Dom would get the benefit of all that sweetness, that shy eagerness to please. He only hoped she had to sense to kick her moronic boyfriend to the curb. Selina deserved better than some prick who was too selfish to give her what she needed.

Brody wrapped his arm around Selina's shoulders and pulled her a little closer. Her cool breath flowed across his chest and he decided it was oddly soothing. Not that he could get used to the sensation or anything. Smiling wryly at his own folly, he closed his eyes and willed himself to sleep.

Selina woke cold and alone, her clothes neatly folded on the chair, no sign that there had ever even been anyone else in the room with her save for the rumpled bed and the musky scent of sex still hanging in the air. Feeling small and abandoned, she wrapped herself in the sheet and looked around. There was a sheet of hotel stationery lying in the middle of the table, a few words scribbled on it in a spiky, masculine hand.

'Look me up if you're ever in Savannah
Brody'

There was a string of numbers after that she recognised as a phone number. With a thoughtful smile, Selina picked the paper up.

I wonder how far it is to Georgia?

CAITLYN LYNCH

Second Surrender

The old van's engine sputtered again, and Selina swore under her breath, taking her foot off the gas.

"There, there, Precious," she murmured, patting the dash. "Not much further..."

"Take the next left," the smooth voice of the navigation program on her phone advised, "Then, your destination is ahead on the left."

"Thank God for that..." but she had perhaps murmured the thanks a little too soon, because she was only halfway through the turn when the engine died completely.

"Oh, crap!"

Brody Cullane looked up from the fence palings he was painting at the sound of a seriously sick vehicle engine in the last throes of dying. The old van was moving pretty slowly, fortunately, because the engine was completely gone as it turned into his street. The brakes apparently went with it, because the van just rolled on steadily through the turn and hit the kerb, the front bumper just grazing a lamp-post.

His instincts had him dropping the brush and darting across the sidewalk, out into the road to yank the driver's door open.

"Hey, are you all right?"

A delicate face with huge doelike brown eyes peered up at him. The owner attempted a sassy smile which came off a little wistful.

"Hi, Brody."

"*Selina?*"

"I'm glad you remember me, or this might turn out even more embarrassing than it already is."

Remember her? He'd never be able to *forget* her. His mind flashed back three months, to a hot night in a Dallas bar and the beautiful girl who'd looked at him with hungry eyes, tempting him. To the way she'd screamed and writhed as he took her, not once but twice, first in a backroom of the bar and later back in his hotel room. Leaving her sleeping in his bed had been one of the toughest things he'd ever had to do.

"What the hell are you doing here?" Brody asked in shock.

"Well, there's only a couple of B. Cullanes in the Savannah phone book and the other one is seventy-three, he made me a cup of tea." Selina smiled up at him, unfastening her seatbelt and slipping out of the van.

Brody was even better-looking than she remembered, she thought, eyeing him up and down. But then, she never had gotten a good look at him in daylight. He looked like he'd been painting, white smears on his fingers and a few speckles on his forearms, shirtless in the hot Georgia sun. Which left his magnificent torso and arm muscles exposed to her greedy eyes.

She was looking at him like she wanted to eat him alive, and Brody's mouth was suddenly dry as his brain decided to replay, in vivid detail, just why he regretted having to leave her behind so badly.

A little thrown by the sudden appearance of the girl who'd haunted his dreams innumerable times since that unforgettable night, he just stood staring down at her in silence. Until her shoulders drooped.

"I see I'm not particularly welcome. Are you married, is that it?" Selina glanced behind him at the house he'd come running from.

"No!" Brody said, startled. Comprehension dawned. "That's why you looked me up and just rocked up, instead of calling, huh?"

She looked down and shrugged a bit sheepishly, scraping the toe of her shoe on the road like a kid caught in mischief. "Not all men wear wedding rings, and I don't want to be a home-wrecker."

"Fair enough." Recovering from his astonishment at last, Brody reached for her hand, enfolded it in his. "Selina, there's no reason why I wouldn't want you here. No reason at all. I'm delighted you decided to surprise me, actually."

Her smile was like the sun coming out.

They left the van parked at the kerb — it was far enough over not to be in anyone's way. Brody figured he'd look at the engine later and see if he could get it running, though it looked like a deathtrap and his protective instincts rebelled at the thought of letting Selina anywhere near it, never mind drive it.

Brody kept on looking down at Selina incredulously as he led her inside; he could hardly believe she'd just turned up. He paused at the fence long enough to put the lid on the paint can and the brush on top.

"Shouldn't you wash that out?" she nodded at the brush.

"It can wait." Opening the screen door, he gestured to her to go in front.

The door opened directly into a huge kitchen/living area. Selina looked around, taking in the polished timber floorboards, the scrubbed pine kitchen benches, the new silver refrigerator. The furniture was plain, utilitarian; the whole place screamed *bachelor*, but a tidy, organised one. The afternoon sun slanted in over the back porch in a bright splash of light, and she felt instantly at home.

"What a lovely house."

"She's my fixer-upper," Brody ran a hand lovingly along the edge of the scrubbed-pine table. "Moved here about a year ago."

"You haven't been on deployment?" Selina wandered over to the window, looked out into a carefully-tended black yard.

"No." He hesitated, before finally lifting one shoulder in a shrug. "I was injured in action two years ago. While it wasn't quite severe enough for them to discharge me, the powers that be decided, in their infinite wisdom, that I'd serve the regiment better from behind a desk these days. They promoted me out of the field."

"You're an officer?" she turned to look at him.

"Lt. Colonel Cullane, at your service, ma'am," he executed a small bow, grinning at her wide eyes.

"That sounds very important," Selina said honestly, and then grinned at him cheekily. "No wonder you're so good at giving orders. Lots of experience."

Brody grinned in return. "And you're an insubordinate little minx who's never been taught the right way to behave." He stalked towards her slowly, giving her plenty of time to edge away if she wanted to, but she didn't move a muscle. Just stood still and tilted her chin up, a little smile playing around the corners of her lips.

Brody didn't touch her. He put his hands on the counter on either side of her instead, looking down at her. She was small enough that the top of her head was on a level with his chin and she had to look way up to meet his eyes.

"Why are you really here, Selina?"

Selina's eyes widened, and then she looked down, apparently thrown by the question. She said nothing, and he, looking down at her, saw her hands clench against her legs.

"Selina," Brody said quietly. She licked her lips convulsively, but still didn't look at him or speak.

"Okay," Brody murmured, seeing that she didn't feel able to talk about it with him in her face like this. Gently, he set his hands on her hips, turned her around. She was wearing a long, flowing cotton skirt and a little top with thin spaghetti straps, leaving her shoulders almost entirely bare. He was tall enough to be able to look down the front of her top and see that she wasn't wearing a bra, her nipples peaked against the thin fabric.

He left his hands on her hips, bent his head to nuzzle lightly at the back of her neck. Her blonde-streaked hair was pinned up in a loose, messy knot, leaving her neck almost entirely exposed. Brody nibbled lightly at Selina's nape, felt goose-bumps spring up. She shivered a little, leaned back towards him, but he moved slightly, not letting her gain any more contact.

"What happened to your bossy jerk of a boyfriend?" he asked quietly.

"He wanted a doormat, not a girlfriend. I got my stuff and I left." Her voice was steady and even.

"You went back there alone?" Brody's protective instincts reared up again.

"I did not. I took my bouncer friend and a couple of his big buddies." Selina's tone was smug.

"And then?"

"Quit work and spent some time disentangling my finances. Worked out my notice while sleeping on a friend's couch."

"And then you left all your friends and your job and drove all the way to Georgia in a rattletrap old van to find me. Tell me why, Selina." He wanted to know, *needed* to know.

"That night," her voice was fainter now, as his lips traced across her shoulder. "That night, I spent with you... it was the only time I've felt truly *alive*, in longer than I can even remember. I don't know if I *ever* felt like that before. I

44

wanted — I wanted to know if it was just a fluke. A one-off."

"You wanted more," at last, he let his hands slip from her hips, sliding forwards around her waist. One of them curving downwards, the other gliding up, beneath the hem of her thin top. "Is that right?"

"Yes," Selina whispered as Brody pressed close against her, the heat of his skin warming her through. One of his big hands pressed over her mound through her skirt, the other traced slowly along the underside of her breasts. She shuddered and tilted her head back against his chest. "Yes, Brody — please."

"I'm glad you came to me, sweetheart," he murmured it quietly against her neck — just before he bit down on the tender flesh below her ear, his hand wrapping around her breast to pinch her nipple firmly between finger and thumb.

Selina moaned with pleasure, sagging limply back against Brody. He felt so good against her, massively strong and protective. She trusted him instinctively, certain that he'd never hurt her — well, not more than she wanted to be hurt, anyway. He was peppering kisses over her neck now, fingers tugging at her nipple, his other hand pressing on her mons pulling her hard back against him so that she could feel his arousal against her ass.

"I've thought about you a lot," Selina confessed breathily. "Dreamed of you, too." She felt him smile against her neck.

"I've thought about you too, sweetheart," he admitted it without shame. "Thought about all the things I wanted to do to you."

She shivered again, her little hands sliding stealthily back behind her, touching his muscled stomach lightly. "I want you — to do all those things."

Brody had to take a couple of slow, deep breaths, steady himself. And then he used his Dom voice, even as he lowered his hands and stepped back from her. "Turn around and take off your clothes."

Selina suppressed a small cry of loss as he moved away, but she was already turning at his command, hands crossing at her waist to grab the hem of her top and peel it up and over her head. She dropped it on the counter behind her, looking up at Brody through her eyelashes. He looked relaxed, one hip perched on the kitchen table, his arms folded across his chest making his muscles bulge thickly as he watched her. Hooking her thumbs in the elastic waist of her skirt, she pushed it down, let it fall to the floor and stepped out of it and her sandals at the same time. Her skimpy panties soon followed, leaving her entirely nude and vulnerable. She had to resist the urge to cross her arms defensively.

"You're even more beautiful than I remembered," Brody said thickly. "Come to me, Selina."

He could tell she was nervous, but she came to him anyway, looking up at him through her lashes, a shy smile on her lips. She looked very young and impossibly beautiful. Brody blew out his cheeks, staring at her.

"If this is just a dream, I really don't wanna

wake up," he muttered.

Selina chuckled, the remark bolstering her confidence. "I could pinch you," she said cheekily.

"Oh, I think it's you who wants to be pinched," his hands flashed out so quickly she gasped; seizing both her nipples, squeezing sharply. She cried out and stumbled forward towards him, her back arching in ecstasy.

"Brody!" There was a frantic plea in her words, one he had no inclination to deny. It was easy for him to twist sideways and push her down onto the table, still tweaking and tugging at her nipples, bending over her to seize one in his mouth and suckle roughly.

Selina moaned, her hands coming up to slide into Brody's short black hair instinctively, before she thought suddenly that he might not like it. He didn't pause in his attentions to her breasts, though, twisting his tongue around one to tug it deep into his mouth as his fingers squeezed the other roughly.

Brody lost himself for several minutes in Selina's breasts, suckling and squeezing, moving from one to the other. Listening to her pleasured moans and luxuriating in the way her short nails scraped at his scalp.

Selina's slender legs wrapped around Brody's torso, holding him close as she arched up against his mouth. He switched breasts again, using his teeth on her nipple this time, biting down until he felt her start to tense, before easing back and soothing the pain with his tongue. Vaguely he thought that he should take her to his bedroom, find some nipple clamps, maybe some other toys she'd like — but right now he wanted to be inside her too badly. He could feel how wet she was, her pussy pressing against his abs, her hips shifting in a desperate attempt to get some friction.

"Brody, please," Selina whimpered, and he couldn't help the possessive growl that escaped him; it really pushed his buttons when she said his name, especially in that breathy, needy tone.

"Gonna give it to you good, sweetheart," he promised, reluctantly pulling off her breasts, straightening up long enough to unfasten his pants and shove them down. He paused then, trying to think if he had a condom in his wallet — *in fact where the hell had he left his wallet?*

Selina let out a little sob, and his aching cock twitched in response. "Selina, I don't think I've got a condom. I'm clean, I promise, don't even remember when I last had sex without one; but are you protected?"

"Pill," she panted, trying to pull him back down to her. "And I got tested when I dumped Mark. Fuck me, Brody, please, want to feel you, feel all of you. Want you to fill me up."

"You could tempt a fuckin' saint," Brody muttered with a rueful grin, but he was inclined to trust her.

Selina thought she might expire from the sheer pleasure as she felt the thick, flared head of Brody's cock pushing at her soaked channel. She'd been thinking about him all day, aroused by the sheer thought of seeing him again, reliving in her mind that one blissful night when he'd ruined her for any other man.

"That's it, beautiful," Brody groaned as she

accepted him, her heels pressing into his ass as she greedily lifted her hips to take him deeper, her hands dropping to the table so she could push herself up to meet his penetration.

"God, you're so tight — so wet..." she felt incredible wrapped around his cock, slick internal muscles tugging on him in a head-spinningly wonderful sensation he suspected was going to make him shoot his load way too fast if he wasn't careful. One strong hand under Selina's ass to hold her at the right height for him, he put the other in between them, rubbing the tip of his thumb roughly over her clit.

Selina's breath came in quick little pants as Brody set up a rhythm, long steady thrusts, almost completely withdrawing before slamming back deep into her. His thumb rotated over her clit in maddening circles, driving her ever closer to climax yet slowing every time she got close, holding her somehow right on the brink.

There was nothing she could do but brace herself against his thrusts. His dark eyes were intent as he stared down at her, his lips parted, white teeth showing in a feral grin as he fucked her long and slow.

"A feast laid out on my kitchen table," Brody said wonderingly, gazing at the beauty spread out under him, very evidently enjoying his attentions. Selina's plump breasts bounced with every thrust, erotic moans sounding out as he worked over her clit with his thumb. "God, you're so lovely. So willing."

She was getting close, he could tell from the way her legs were starting to shake, her eyelids to flutter. "That's it. That's it," he crooned, speeding up his thrusts suddenly, rewarded as Selina came apart with a throaty scream of his name. "Good girl, such a good girl, Jesus that feels so good," he couldn't hold out against her as viselike muscles tightened convulsively on his throbbing cock. "Fuuuuck!"

Selina cried out with renewed pleasure as heat flooded deep inside her, Brody bending over her, holding her tightly against him as his hot seed spurted into Selina's receptive body. She reached up blindly, clung to his broad shoulders as they both shook with reaction.

Brody sought her mouth with his, and Selina smiled against his lips as he kissed her, stubble rasping on her tender skin. "Thank you," she whispered when he lifted his head a little.

"Thank *me*? Thank *you*," he said with a quiet chuckle. "Trust me, it really isn't every Sunday afternoon a gorgeous girl like you has her van break down outside my house and comes in for fun and games on my kitchen table. You're the first."

That made Selina giggle, and Brody caught his breath as her muscles squeezed down on him again. "Damn, girl," he murmured, seeking her mouth again. She stroked his neck and shoulders as they kissed, a soft, delicate touch that was more tenderness anyone had shown Brody Cullane in longer than he could remember.

A warning voice in the back of his head whispered *don't get addicted, don't do it*, but for now at least he was able to drown it out, just luxuriating in the feeling of Selina's gentle hands on his skin.

Selina sighed with loss as Brody pulled back from her. She felt wet and sticky between her thighs; pushing herself upwards she asked;

"Bathroom?"

"First on the right," Brody said, pointing along the hall. She nodded and hurried off, suddenly feeling embarrassed about being nude in front of him.

The bathroom was neat and clean for a bachelor — in fact the whole house was immaculate, Selena mused, taking a quick shower and borrowing one of the neatly folded towels on the counter to dry off with. Must be Brody's military habits, flowing over into his personal life. *An officer. He's very good at giving orders...* she shivered with anticipation, her mouth suddenly dry.

"Selina," a tap on the door made her start and clutch at the towel.

"Come in," she called, before she could think better of it. The door opened to reveal Brody standing there. He looked her over for a moment, wrapped in the towel, her hair hanging wetly down her back. His eyes darkened, but he only said;

"I brought you this to wear. If you like." He held out a folded, faded chambray shirt.

She bit on her lip, staring up at him wide-eyed, before taking it from his hand, saying "Thank you," in a small voice.

The very thought of seeing Selina wear his shirt — and he'd deliberately given her the one he'd been wearing earlier, so that it would have his scent on it — was making his hunger for her peak again. He backed out of the bathroom slowly. It was an actual struggle to make himself shut the door; but he couldn't intrude on her privacy that way, no matter how much the thought tempted him.

Not yet, anyway. She hadn't given him permission to invade her personal space that far.

Still, he couldn't make himself move away from the door; so when Selina came out she found him leaning against the wall opposite, arms folded across his broad chest, his eyes tracing slowly over her from head to bare toes and back again, lingering on her bare, slender legs.

"Fucking hell, but you're beautiful," Brody said, making Selina blush shyly and look down at her feet. He unfolded his arms and reached out, one huge hand cupping her cheek gently. "Don't do that, don't look away. You're stunning, Selina, and I'm gonna keep telling you that until you believe it. Until you have the confidence you *should* have."

He bent his head to take her lips in a deep, possessive kiss, one muscled arm curling around her waist and pulling her close, his hand sliding into her hair and holding her head still as he plundered her mouth again.

"I should... probably get my clothes and go," Selina murmured when he finally let her go.

"No," Brody didn't even think twice. "Where are you going to go?" he tried to moderate his voice, realizing he'd instinctively slipped into his commanding Dom voice, and he didn't have the right to command Selina. She wasn't *his*.

Not yet, the little voice in his head whispered

again.

"Well, I figured I'd try to get the van up and running again," Selina shrugged, and Brody's eyes were magnetically drawn to her shoulder as his shirt slid down, baring it.

"And then what?" he couldn't seem to pull his eyes away from that slim bare shoulder. "What are your plans? Where are you headed?"

She didn't answer, her gaze sliding away from his. "Nowhere in particular."

A sudden suspicion came to him. "Selina — have you been *living* in that van? Holy Christ, you have!" when she wouldn't meet his eyes. He reached out to grasp her shoulders, feeling with horror their fragility, the delicacy of her form. "*Anything* could have happened to you!"

"But it didn't," she whispered, huge doe-like eyes flickering up to meet his at last. "I'm safe, Brody. With you."

They stared at each other for a long moment before Brody said quietly "Stay, Selina. For a while, at least. Until you have a plan for what you want to do. I can help you find work — help you fix up that rattletrap van, too. Just... stay. Please."

Her eyes searched his face, and he wondered what she was looking for. He'd made it a request; would she be more likely to give in if he tried to command her? While that was apparently what she needed in the bedroom, he suspected it would only drive her away if he tried to boss her around outside it.

Finally, her sweet smile blossomed, and she said "Okay. Thank you."

"Good." He nodded decisively, wondering

what the hell it was about this girl that made him feel like an awkward teenager. "Your van, though. I 'spect you have some stuff in it that you want, and we should get it off the road — if you steer, I can probably push it up on the driveway even if we can't get it to start."

She smiled at his take-charge attitude, nodded in agreement. Except... "Won't that block your garage? Do you need to get your car out first?"

"I don't have a car," he shook his head, reaching for her hand and leading her towards the door. He'd put her shoes there and she stepped into them as he stooped to pull his trainers on.

"Oh," she stopped, looking up at him. "*Tell* me you ride a motorbike. Please."

"Would you like that?" he grinned, tugging lightly on her hand to lead her down the steps.

"So hot," Selina sighed, following him to the van. "Please tell me you'll take me for a ride."

"Oh, baby," the grin he gave her was pure heat. "The ride of your life."

The van wouldn't start, but Brody found it easy enough, with Selina steering, to push it onto his level driveway.

"Pop the hood!" he called to her as she set the parking brake. One look under the van's hood had him shaking his head. "How the hell did you get this all the way here from Texas?" he asked incredulously as Selina joined him at the front of the van.

She smiled and shrugged, patting the bumper. "She might be old, but she's done me good service, I promise you."

"I think it might be time to give the old girl an honorable retirement, though," Brody shook his head again. "I'll talk to a buddy of mine, works on the motor pool at the base. One of his crack mechanics might get it up and running again."

"You don't have to do that," Selina protested.

"I want to do that." Looking down at her, he maneuvered to lean over her, pressing her back against the side of the van. "I want to make sure you're safe." His eyes blazed down at her before he leaned in to claim another kiss.

Selina's arms came up to tentatively clutch at his shoulders, her mouth softly opening under his. She made delightful little noises when he kissed her, Brody discovered; soft sounds in the back of her throat that made him hungry for her again already.

"Get your stuff," he pulled back at last. "I've got plenty of space in my closet. C'mon."

He was appalled to see how little she actually had, considering that the van appeared to contain the entirety of her worldly possessions. Apart from a rather elderly laptop and a pair of cheap speakers, there was a small box of well-thumbed books and a couple of bags of clothes.

"That's it?" he said disbelievingly as she dropped the second holdall at his feet and hopped out of the van, pushing her hair back behind her ears.

Selina shrugged. "I don't need much. I'm pretty low-maintenance," she looked up, eyes fixing appealingly on his. "I won't get in your way, Brody, I promise, and I'll be gone as soon as you're tired of me..."

"Can't see that happening any time soon,

honestly," he shouldered the bag and reached for her hand. He'd already taken the other things inside while she gathered the rest of her clothes. "Come on. Let me show you around, and we should probably get some food into you. Why am I suspecting that the cup of tea the other Mr. Cullane gave you was the only thing you've had all day?"

"It wasn't!" Selina protested. "I had breakfast!"

"And it's now almost six, so that cup of tea was lunch, was it?"

She mumbled something.

"I'm sorry, I didn't catch that?"

"I was too nervous about seeing you again to eat," she blurted, and Brody tipped his head back and groaned.

"You didn't seriously think I wouldn't be happy to see you?"

"I didn't know!" Selina confessed. "I didn't know anything about you except that you were a soldier and the town you lived in... I... I... you could have been married or anything..."

"Shh," he comforted her gently, seeing that she was nearly in tears. Leading her into his bedroom, he sat down on the bed and pulled her into his lap. "There's no-one else in my life, Selina. I'm not the kind of man who would cheat on a girl, I promise you." There was something dark in his voice, but he went on before she could ask what he meant. "But I am a Dom, and any woman who wanted to be in my life long-term would need to be a submissive, at least in my bed. I don't think I could settle for less."

She nodded against his neck. "I understand. I

didn't, before I met you, but — I've been reading up. You were right about me. About what I need."

"But you don't need it out of bed," he tried to explain. "So many subs do, they're needy for attention constantly, and I'm a soldier. I've spent the last fifteen years deployed for months or years at a time to various sand-filled hellholes. It's tough on the ones left behind, the wives and girlfriends. A needy sub just wouldn't cope."

"I see," Selina was watching his face, listening intently.

"But," he traced a thumb lightly down her cheek, "I don't think you're like that. That kind of sub wouldn't have looked at me the way you did in that nightclub."

She laughed at that, casting her long lashes down shyly.

"And even if you were, my overseas combat days are over. I'm a desk warrior these days. I'll be here for you if you need me, Selina, I promise you."

"Oh," she said softly, looking up at him again, "I need you, Brody. Very much."

There wasn't a whole lot he could say to that, because the sensual promise in her tone had completely scrambled his brain. So instead he pulled her down on the bed beside him and unbuttoned his shirt, kissing her soft skin as he bared it.

"I have some toys I think you'll like," he murmured, kissing his way across her stomach. "Shall I get them out?"

"I don't know," Selina gasped as his strong

fingers latched onto her nipples, tugging and twisting. "Teach me, Brody. Teach me what you want me to do."

"I want you to have the time of your life," he answered with a low chuckle, before letting go of her reluctantly and standing up. "All right. Let's play a game."

Shrugging off the unbuttoned shirt, she lay back and smiled up at him. "What sort of game?"

"This one's called *how many times can Selina come*." He smirked down at her before reaching to the nightstand and pulling open the bottom drawer. "Let's see. Ah yes, you'll look so pretty in these. On your knees, angel." The last few words were said in his Dom voice, and he watched with intense satisfaction as she got immediately to her knees, sitting back on her heels, hands behind her back.

Selina waited trustingly for Brody to show her what he held in his hands. He knelt on the bed before her, leaning in to kiss her, biting lightly at her lower lip, tugging on it. She lost herself in the sensation until she felt him tug sharply at one of her sensitive, aching nipples — and then there was a slowly increasing pressure that made her gasp and shudder.

"Remember your colors," Brody pulled back from the kiss and looked closely at Selina. Her mouth hung open, soft panting breaths making her chest heave.

"G-green," she panted, so he tightened the screw on the nipple clamp, slowly, watching her all the while. "Ah, ah, yellow!"

"Okay," he turned the screw back a half turn.

"That better?"

"Yes — yes, feels so good, Brody!"

"Good girl." He kissed her again, reached for the other breast. The silver clamps were connected by a fine chain; it trembled as she shuddered with reaction, dangling down towards her belly button. Hooking a finger through it once he had the second nipple clamp attached to his satisfaction, he tugged lightly.

Selina let out a little sobbing sound that might have been his name, swaying towards him. Her eyes had glazed over with lust, making Brody groan at how gorgeous she looked.

"Good girl," he crooned softly, "what a good, beautiful girl. Time for you to get me hard again so I can give you what you need."

Standing up beside the bed, he unzipped and removed his shorts, reached out to guide her closer to him. "Just the way you like to do it, baby," he encouraged softly, running his thumb over her bottom lip gently. She tongued and sucked at it, making him smile. "That's it, show me what you want to do. Such a good girl."

She had a praise kink, he thought, as she moaned at his words, sucking his thumb deeper into her mouth, flicking her tongue quickly over the pad. He used his free hand to pet her hair lightly, calling her a good girl again before gently pulling his hand out of her mouth.

"Come on now, baby, I got something else here that needs sucking." His cock was already stirring with interest, barely an hour after he'd pumped himself dry inside her. Just like last time, he thought with a grin as she leaned forward to place kisses over his abs, working her way down towards his cock.

"May I use my hand?" Selina begged, her voice soft and a little dreamy.

"You may, but it's that hot little mouth I really want to feel," Brody told her, staring down at her as she moved, the chain hanging from her nipples swinging. Before she touched him, he reached down quickly to grab the chain, lifting it up above his cock. Tugging lightly as her little pink tongue flicked out to trace the sensitive ridge of skin at the tip of his cock.

Selina gasped as he tugged and a little shock raced through her from her aching nipples. She looked up to meet Brody's eyes, warm and approving as he gazed down at her, one hand still stroking her hair gently.

"You are so lovely," he said softly.

Eager to please him, she opened her mouth and sucked the head of his cock in, hollowing her cheeks and taking in as much as she could without gagging. Wrapping one hand around the base of his cock, she reached under to stroke his balls with the other, rolling them in her fingers.

"Huhhh," Brody groaned, but he was careful not to tighten his fingers in Selina's hair, as his cock thickened and lengthened in her mouth and she had to pull back to avoid choking, lips sliding wetly along his length. "That's it," he breathed, stroking her hair with his hand, running his fingers through the silken strands. Twitching the chain in his other hand in gentle, rhythmic tugs, setting the rhythm for her to suck on him, her mouth sliding over the end of his cock, tongue lapping thirstily at the pre-cum beading on the tip.

Selina breathed in quick, panting breaths through her nose as Brody pulled gently on the chain on her nipples. His cock was fully hard again and leaking; eagerly she tried to take him a little deeper into her throat but he tugged on her hair gently, pulling her back. The pull on her hair combined with the tug on her clamped nipples dragged a high, frantic whine from her throat and a chuckle from Brody.

"You like this, baby?"

She nodded frantically as he drew her mouth off his cock.

"Good. I've got another toy for you, too. Stay right there." Letting go of her hair and the chain, he took hold of her wrists gently, pressed her hands down against her thighs. "Right there, honey. Just leave them right there."

"Please," she whimpered. "So wet, Brody, want you to touch me..."

"Patience," he said softly, stepping back to admire her, the chain swinging as she panted, the weight tugging at her nipples. There was a delicious flush of arousal from her breasts all the way up to her face. "So fucking pretty," Brody murmured, turning back to the drawer he kept his toys in to select another. "Close your eyes, Selina. I want this one to be a surprise."

He used his Dom voice, pleased to see that she obeyed instantly, even in her aroused state. A fine tremor set up in her muscles, though, and he thought that she was dropping fast into subspace. Getting onto the bed beside her, he placed one hand firmly on her shoulder to anchor her. "You with me here, Selina? Give me a colour."

It took her several long moments, him steadying her with that one firm hand, before she was able to pant out "Green."

"Do you need to open your eyes?"

"N-no."

"All right." Leaning in, he placed slow, nibbling kisses up the side of her neck, before catching her earlobe in his teeth and tugging gently. She leaned back towards him with a soft sigh, her shoulders pressing against his chest. "Stay with me," Brody said in his Dom voice, "I need you to keep giving me a colour, okay?"

"C-can I have a colour for 'please give me more, you're going too slow'?" Selina moaned, making him laugh, surprised and pleased.

"Ah, the anticipation will make it all the sweeter, beautiful," he kissed her hair. "I'll take care of you, don't you worry about that." His hand smoothed down over her bottom, slipped between the pert cheeks and teased forward to her pussy. "My, you *are* wet, aren't you?"

Selina moaned, shifting, trying to push herself back onto his fingers. He chuckled, withdrew his hand and dealt her ass a sharp little smack. "Am I going to have to teach you a lesson about being patient, hmm?"

She'd let out a tiny scream as he smacked her, an erotic little wail that made him suddenly hungry to hear more. "Put your hands on the bed and lean forward," he ordered hoarsely. She obeyed immediately, and his lust rose as he stared down at her presented so perfectly for him.

He didn't spank her bottom again

immediately, though, and Selina made a grumpy sound and wiggled her ass, trying to tempt him. Brody only laughed, though.

"*Patience,*" he told her. "Gotta juuuust do this first..."

Eyes closed, forehead resting on her crossed forearms, Selina couldn't figure out what he was waiting for. She heard a click, a wet sound — and then something pressed firmly against the puckered little rosebud of her ass.

"Colour," Brody demanded as he pushed the plug in a little way. He'd chosen a small one for her this first time, tapering in after the widest point before flaring out to a wide, flat base.

"Green," Selina gasped as he pushed a little further. It must have been lube that he was putting on the plug while he told her to wait, she realised; it was sliding in slickly with little pressure from Brody. "Oh God, oh God, yel-ahhh!" She'd started to say *yellow* as he got to the widest point, she realised, and then suddenly the pressure eased as the plug popped inside her.

"Hold still, just take a moment to get used to it," Brody murmured, hand smoothing over her lower back. "Does it feel good, baby?"

She couldn't speak. Could only moan and shift under his hand, so full and yet utterly *empty*, needing *more*. Sneakily, she attempted to slip a hand between her thighs, touch her throbbing clit.

"Oh, no you don't," Brody had been waiting for just such a move. In a moment he had hold of Selina's wrist, bringing it to the small of her back. "Naughty girl. I told you, you wait until I say so."

"Please," Selina whimpered, and then she shrieked loudly as Brody's hand came down sharply on her ass — on the plug in her ass, shifting it inside her even as his palm stung her tender skin. "Oh God yes, please do that again!" she shouted. Heard Brody's rough chuckle just before the second spank landed, this one a little lower, his fingers curving upwards so that his fingertips slapped against her pussy, the heel of his hand hitting the base of the plug and jolting it inside her ass.

Selina saw stars, screams of pleasure spilling from her as she jerked, but it wasn't *enough*, she knew it wouldn't be enough even though it felt so insanely good. Her clamped nipples were rubbing against the bedsheet beneath her, sending little shocks of pain/pleasure through her body with each strike of Brody's hand.

He kept the slaps light and carefully targeted, the tip of his middle finger just making contact with her clit with each stroke. His other hand holding her wrist at the small of her back kept her steady and still as he worked her up higher and higher.

And then he *stopped*, leaving her teetering on the edge, sobbing his name amidst hoarse pleas.

"Colour, sweetheart," Brody requested, but Selina was too far gone. She could only shake and sob;

"Please, Brody, *please*! I need it, I need you, oh please..."

"I got you," he soothed, letting her wrist go. Sitting down on the edge of the bed and picking her up, her slight form nothing to his strength, settling her on his lap, her back to his chest. "All right, honey. Take what you want."

She scrabbled frantically at his thighs, pushing herself up and easing back, taking the thickly swollen head of his cock into her pussy and sinking down with a low, guttural moan of fulfilment.

"That what you needed, sweetheart?" Brody murmured in her ear.

"So full," she whimpered in response, finding that having him pushed deep inside her this way also put a delicious pressure on the plug in her ass.

"I know. Told you you'd like it. You feel so tight." He lifted his hands to her breasts, flicked his fingertips very lightly over her nipples. "These must be really aching by now."

Selina's panting breaths came even quicker as he gently released the clamps, massaging the crushed points gently with his fingertips as the blood rushed back into them. Her body arched back, breasts thrusting forward into his hands — and she came, her pussy clenching and tightening on his cock in a blissful pull and tug that had Brody groaning deep in his chest with pleasure.

"Aww, yeah," he groaned against her neck, his hips rocking as he thrust up into her. He released one breast, dropped his hand to thrum his fingers over her clit, prolonging her orgasm, driving her mercilessly back up towards another peak as she started to come down.

"Grab your nipples," he ordered breathlessly in her ear, releasing her other breast. "Tug on 'em."

Selina made a frantic little sobbing sound, but she did exactly as she was told, catching her nipples between finger and thumb and tugging, squeezing. Watching over her shoulder, Brody thought he'd never seen anything so erotic in his life. He could feel his own climax approaching, feel his balls pulling up to his body and tightening, the tingle at the base of his spine.

"That's it. That's it," he groaned, using his free hand to clamp her hip, holding her steady as he pistoned hard up into her, fingers all the time working over her soaked, slippery clit.

Writhing on the thick impalement of Brody's cock, Selina cried out his name over and over again. She'd never felt anything so good in her life, the sting of where he'd slapped her bottom rubbing on his hard thighs, her aching nipples unbearably stimulated, her clit swollen and throbbing. She was pretty sure that she could have come again even without his fingers rubbing that incredibly sensitive spot — but with them, it was inevitable, and sooner rather than later.

She felt his breathing change, his thrusts become deeper and yet more erratic, gloried in the thought that he must be enjoying this very nearly as much as she was. His strong fingers pinched at her clit suddenly and Selina was lost; screaming out her ecstasy even as Brody pumped himself dry in her convulsing pussy with a roar of triumph.

Stunned and exhausted, Selina collapsed to her stomach on the bed as Brody eased out of her, lifting her and laying her down. His strong hand smoothed over her back gently, and then she felt him turning her over, arranging her comfortably on the bed. He said something, but she was too out of it to understand the words. Only when she felt a warm damp cloth wiping between her legs did she rouse a little, blinking blearily up at him.

"Hush, angel," Brody said softly, "just cleaning you up a little." Her pupils were dilated and she was a little shocky, he thought; discarding the cloth onto the floor for now he climbed into bed beside her and pulled the cover over both of them, holding her close and murmuring soothing words of praise into her ear until her shivering stopped and she moved a little closer to him, nestling her face into his neck.

"I'll have to shave for you," he murmured, "or you'll get terrible stubble rash, your skin's so tender."

He felt her smile against his throat, the soft kiss she placed in the hollow, before she said softly "I don't mind. I like the marks you leave on me."

That thought was so hot he groaned again. "Say things like that and I'll be cuffing you to my bed to keep you here permanently."

"I don't think I'd mind that either," she admitted with a little giggle.

"God, it's like you were invented just to tempt me." Rolling her to her back, bracing himself above her, he kissed her long and slow. "Stay here and rest a little while, hmm? I'll go make us something to eat."

"I could help..." she offered, but he shook his head.

"You stay there. The price of me getting to dominate you is that I have to take care of you afterwards, and it's a price that I'm more than happy to pay for you, Selina."

Recognising that this was something he felt he needed to do, Selina smiled and snuggled down among the bedcovers he tucked around her after getting out of bed. He pressed a light kiss on her brow before pulling his shorts back on and leaving the room.

She must have drowsed off, warm and comfortable in a proper bed for the first time in weeks, because the next thing she knew Brody was shaking her gently awake and the room was dim with oncoming twilight.

"Hey, baby. You ready to eat?"

"Sure," she realised she was hungry, climbed out of bed and let him put his shirt back on her, smiling at the warmly possessive look in his eyes as he buttoned it up. Taking her hand, he led her back to the kitchen, where a delicious little feast was laid out awaiting them.

"Oh, how lovely," Selina gasped, looking at the table — the very table where Brody had fucked her so deliciously roughly only a couple of hours ago. He'd spread a checked cloth over it, lit a couple of white pillar candles, and laid out plates, wine glasses and a bottle of wine. A bowl of *pasta carbonara* steamed in the middle of the table, the scent augmented by the freshly baked garlic bread beside it.

Suddenly realising just how ravenous she was, Selina accepted the seat Brody held out for her, let him serve her a heaping plate of pasta and tore off a thick chunk of garlic bread to go with it.

Brody watched as Selina tucked in hungrily, smiling to himself. It took him a little while to realise that the warm feeling in the pit of his stomach wasn't from the hot meal they were sharing, but from an emotion so unfamiliar it took him a while to recognise it.

Contentment.

Brody was giving her the strangest look. Selina got the feeling that she was too much in his space, just turning up and thrusting herself into his life. A little uncomfortable under his intense scrutiny, she shifted about slightly before eventually saying;

"The food's wonderful, Brody, thank you so much."

"You're welcome," he blinked and seemed to shake himself out of whatever mood had come over him. Smiling broadly then, he leaned forward, took her hand and said "Selina, I can't tell you how happy I am that you're here. Seeing you is the best surprise I've had in, I can't even tell you how long."

Her smile as she beamed back at him was like being bathed in warm sunlight.

"I'm so glad you said that. You'd gone quiet and I was just thinking that maybe I'm intruding..."

"Never," he said with quiet passion, squeezing her fingers gently. "You're welcome here as long as you want to stay, Selina. I promise you that."

Reassured, she squeezed his hand back. "Oh, I think you'll get sick of me sooner or later."

"Never happen." Grinning at her, he lifted the

bottle of wine to top up her glass. "I do have to go to work tomorrow, though. Will you be okay to stay here on your own, with your van not running? I'll leave you a key, and there's a convenience store about ten minutes' walk away, it's a pretty safe area..."

"Sounds lovely," she said positively.

"And I'll see if my buddy from the motor pool can send someone out to pick up the van. They'll tow it into the workshop for a look."

"I think it would probably cost more than it's worth to fix it," Selina said doubtfully.

"You'd be surprised. I've seen those boys cobble together entire vehicles out of bits of scrap lying around the workshops. Let them have a look, huh?"

"All right," she acquiesced with a smile -- followed by an intense yawn, which made Brody laugh.

"I've worn you out, huh?"

"Mm," she admitted, "but I'm enjoying just spending time with you. And drinking this lovely wine."

"Finish your glass off, then, and turn in." She'd eaten everything on her plate, he was pleased to note. "I'll clean up."

Selina was too tired to protest, and really, it was absolutely lovely to be pampered. Especially when he carried her back to bed and tucked her in. She woke once in the night, at first startled to find herself in an unfamiliar place, but she was spooned into the curve of Brody's bigger body, one thickly muscled arm tucked around her waist, his warm breath slow and steady against her neck as he slept.

Relaxing into him with a blissfully content sigh, Selina closed her eyes again.

Selina woke alone, but with a note on the bedside table from Brody, a key to the front door folded up inside, that said he'd be back around four. Stretching luxuriously in the sinfully comfortable bed, she looked at the clock and was surprised to see it was almost ten already.

"Enough idling in bed, Selina my girl," she told herself sternly, "if you're going to impose on Brody's hospitality, the least you can do is earn your keep!" Scrambling out of bed, she hurried to the bathroom. She'd start with a shower, she thought, and then investigate what she could make them for dinner. Since Brody cooked the previous night, and cleaned up, she reckoned it was her turn.

It was just after four when she heard the rumble of a motorbike coming along the street. Running to the bedroom window, she peered out, sighed with lust as she saw Brody manoeuvring a big Harley into his garage. Smiling to herself, she hurried to the bed to complete the last of her preparations.

Brody opened the front door to be greeted by the scent of something absolutely delicious. Following his nose to the kitchen, he found a casserole slow-cooking in a crockpot, cheese dumplings floating on the top, the savoury smell making his mouth water.

"Wow, Selina," he mumbled, turned to look for her. "You here, baby?" he called when he didn't spot her at once.

"In here!" her voice called from the bedroom.

Smiling, he headed over — and stopped dead in the doorway, feasting his eyes ravenously on the sight that greeted him.

Selina lay on her back on the bed, wearing a black lace basque with garters, fishnet stockings and panties that were little more than a wisp of fabric. The bra cups were tugged down to reveal her nipples, to which she'd already attached his clamps — and her hands were secured to his sturdy wooden bedframe by a pair of padded handcuffs secured around her slim wrists.

"Well, this is an even better surprise than yesterday's," Brody said when he recovered his voice. "Checked out my bottom drawer, did you, angel?"

She smiled up at him as he came to stand beside her, his dark eyes running slowly over her, taking in every inch of what she was offering up. "You were the one who suggested cuffing me to your bed and keeping me, and I realised that I rather liked the idea of being restrained and at your mercy." Deliberately, she fluttered her eyelashes at him, licked her lips. "Whatever *will* you do with me?" she asked breathily.

"I don't know what I want to do first, honestly, you're such a temptation," he started unbuttoning his shirt as he spoke, shucked it carelessly, bent to unlace his boots. "Wait," he paused, arrested by an idea. "Aha. I do know what to do with you first, you tempting little minx."

He dived into that bottom drawer full of fascinating toys again. Selina didn't even know what half of them were for — including the egg-shaped device he pulled out.

"What *is* that?" she asked curiously.

Brody smirked, leaning over her. "You're about to find out. Let that keep you busy for a little while," and he switched it on and tucked it into her panties.

"Oh God," Selina soon found that the vibrations from the egg were enough to stimulate her intensely, but not quite get her to orgasm. She writhed desperately around on the bed, unable to move far because of her restrained hands, broken little whimpers and please spilling out of her as Brody took his time getting undressed, enjoying watching her fall apart.

"You doing okay there, baby?" he knelt beside her on the bed, curved a hand over her mons to press the vibrator a bit more firmly against her clit.

"I want to come, Brody please let me come," Selina sobbed.

"Not just yet, angel. Want to feel you come on my cock."

"Oh yes, yes, please, I want that too," she begged, so he took the egg out and switched it off, tugged her panties aside and entered her with one long, smooth thrust.

Selina's back bowed, her legs wrapped around his waist as she strained up towards him, moaning throatily for more.

"You're a greedy little wench," Brody chuckled, his voice a little tight as he felt the first faint flutters of her internal muscles beginning to clench around him. He flexed his hips to push in a little further, groaned with pleasure as she tightened down hard on him, heels digging into his ass. "That's it, baby, take it all. God, look at you," she was absolutely stunning as she climaxed, her pretty mouth open in an O, eyes closed, slender neck arched. He couldn't resist leaning in to give her a hickey on that smooth pale throat, savouring the way she clenched around him and moaned, her orgasm going on and on until finally she stilled with a long sigh.

"So lovely," Brody muttered, drinking her in with his eyes, the way her eyelashes fluttered open and she smiled dreamily up at him. "You love this, don't you? Love getting fucked."

"Only by you," she murmured, perfectly truthfully. "It's never been like this for me with anyone else, Brody. Only you."

"Gonna take care of you," Brody muttered, somewhat awed by the confession. "Gonna make sure it's always good for you, angel."

She gave him the most adorable little smirk, and squeezed her legs a little tighter around his waist, bucking her hips up. "Go on then."

"You little minx," he had to laugh, but then sobered. "You want some more, huh? Greedy girl. All right, I got what you need." He sat back on his heels, strong hands clasping her hips to pull her up into his lap, her shoulders and head still down on the mattress.

"Oh God," Selina groaned as the shift in position pushed the tip of his cock up at a sharper angle inside her, put direct pressure on her G-spot. Her small hands clawed at the timber bedpost she'd cuffed herself to as Brody pounded into her hard, ecstatic screams spilling from her lips as he drove her rapidly back up towards that sharp edge of ecstasy again.

"Come on, angel, come on, come on!" Brody urged fiercely, hammering even harder into her, bringing one hand forward to chafe his tum roughly over her clit. "That's it, yes, *yeahhh*," as her eyelids fluttered and she groaned deep in her throat. Sleek wet muscles clenched around his cock in a blissful ripple of sensation that made Brody's eyes roll back in his head. He shouted her name in bliss as his own climax roared through him, hot spurts of his seed jetting up his cock to spray deep inside Selina's willing, grasping pussy.

Bracing his arms to avoid collapsing atop Selina, Brody kissed her tenderly. She opened her eyes and smiled up at him, gasping as he reached to gently remove her nipple clamps, one at a time, sucking each abused nub of flesh into his mouth for a long, soothing suckle.

At last he lifted his head to look up at her, at her still-restrained hands, her beautiful brown eyes gazing at him.

"I really, really liked my coming-home-from-work present," he told her.

Selina chuckled. "There's more, you know. I made dinner."

"I know. I saw the crock-pot. It smells wonderful, even better now I've worked up an appetite." Easing carefully out of her, he picked up the handcuff key from the nightstand, unlocked the cuffs and took her wrists in his hands, massaging them gently. "But you don't have to do that, Selina. Or this, delightful as it is," he gestured at her body in the sexy lingerie. "I don't want or need any sort of payment for you staying here. There's no strings attached…"

She pulled one hand from his, put soft fingers to his cheek. "I know, Brody. I *wanted* to do it. Cook dinner for you and," she blushed rosily, "be here for you to — *play* with when you got home."

Gazing down at her, he turned his head to kiss at her fingers. "I promise you, I will never, ever complain if you take it into your head to surprise me like this again. I just don't want you to feel *obliged* to."

"Okay." Her cheeky smile flashed. "Well, I don't want you to feel *obliged* to screw me silly if you happen to come home and find me chained to your bed again, either."

Brody couldn't help but laugh, rolling to his side and gathering her into his arms for a close cuddle. "I seriously doubt I'd ever be able to fucking resist that, angel."

"Then I shall be sure to keep doing it."

He couldn't resist kissing her again for the sassy remark, and she twined herself around him and kissed him back.

"But seriously, Brody," Selina said softly when their lips parted, "thanks for letting me stay."

"As long as you want, angel," he told her quietly, sincerely. "As long as you want."

Third Thrills

Selina waved merrily to one of Brody's neighbors as she rode by. The woman waved back with a friendly smile, quite accustomed by now to seeing Selina ride past on her bike on her way to and from work.

A little over two months since Selina had turned up unexpectedly on Brody Cullane's doorstep, she felt as though she'd been living in the area all her life. Several of Brody's brother officers in the Rangers lived on the surrounding streets and she'd been immediately befriended by their wives and girlfriends, all of them happy to welcome the newcomer in their midst. She'd quickly found a part-time job, four mornings a week as a receptionist in a local doctor's office, and contributed the entirety of her earnings into a joint household account she and Brody had set up to share grocery bills and the like — even though Brody tried to insist she needn't at first, he'd soon given in when she insisted. Selina might be a submissive in the bedroom but she was no-one's kept woman.

Even her old van was gone, fixed up by the base's mechanics and sold to a teenager who wanted to do some traveling. Selina didn't miss it. Humming to herself, she wheeled her bike up to Brody's garage and took it inside, locking the door behind her as she came out.

She was just climbing the porch steps to the house, thinking about what she might cook for dinner that evening, when the sound of a car pulling into the driveway behind her made her turn in surprise. Brody wasn't due home for a while yet, and he'd be on his Harley, anyway.

Her lips parted in surprise at the sight of the car; a gleaming silver-gray convertible Porsche, the roof down, the driver a handsome blond man who gave her a broad smile as he got out of the car. He was wearing Air Force dress uniform, all gleaming gold braid and buttons. Selina had learned to read Army insignia easily, but the only thing she could tell about this Air Force officer was that he had fewer stripes on his sleeves than Brody, a Lieutenant-Colonel, and was therefore probably of lesser rank. And the medals on the breast of his jacket were a scant three rows, as compared to the ten rows of Brody's. Whoever this pretty boy was, he hadn't seen much in the way of combat.

"Good afternoon," she said politely.

"Hi there!" the blond's smile really was rather gorgeous, though, she thought. "You must be Selina, lovely to meet you. I'm Chad Marshall."

She stared blankly at him as he came up the

steps, hand outstretched to shake. He tilted his head, smile firmly in place.

"Chad? Brody's brother?"

Selina couldn't hide her astonishment. "Brody never mentioned that he had a brother!"

"He never mentioned that his girlfriend was such a stunner, either, but I can actually sympathize with him on that. He'd be scared I'd come by and try to steal you away." Chad grinned at her, and she found herself laughing. Accepting his offered hand, she shook.

"Please do come in. Brody should be back in an hour or so. Can you stay — will you have dinner with us?"

"That's a very kind invitation," he smiled down at her, gallantly opening the door and holding it for her after she unlocked it. "I'd be delighted."

She led him through to the kitchen, put the coffee machine on. "So, are you older or younger than Brody?" He looked younger, though honestly he looked nothing like Brody at all, lean and blond where Brody was dark and stocky.

"Five years younger," Chad replied, watching Selina as she moved gracefully around the kitchen making coffee, fetching out a cookie jar and setting it on the table before him with an inviting smile. He noted everything about her carefully; her lithe, slender grace, the way her voice softened and she smiled when she said Brody's name.

Chad also noticed the hickey revealed to his curious gaze as the collar of her blouse shifted a little, and the faint marks around her wrists that spoke of restraints regularly applied. He smiled slightly to himself.

"So how come you're Air Force while Brody's in the Army?" Selina's brow wrinkled curiously. "I thought families tended to stick with the same branch of the armed forces?"

"Brody's the rebel," Chad said with a shrug. "Dad was in the Air Force until he retired and went into politics. I think Brody joined the Army just to spite him, frankly. Typical Brody."

Selina didn't think it sounded like Brody at all, but — who was she to argue with his own brother? It still seemed a bit odd to her that Brody had never mentioned even *having* a brother, but then, thinking back, she couldn't remember him ever talking about his family at all. His father was a *politician*?

"How do you like your coffee?" she asked with a hospitable smile, resolving to press Brody on the issue later. Some deep instinct was warning her against confiding too much in Chad.

"Black and strong," Chad answered, making her smile widen a little, because that was exactly how Brody took his coffee too. "And please, Selina, won't you sit down and tell me a little about yourself? Brody's been keeping you all to himself, and I for one have been dying to meet the woman who's captured my wayward brother's heart."

She blushed and laughed a little. "Oh, I don't know about that — we haven't been seeing each other all that long," she prevaricated. "And I'm not very interesting, besides. I'd far rather hear about what Brody was like as a kid."

"A little terror. But I'm sure you could have

guessed that." Chad's megawatt smile flashed again.

He was funny, witty and charming, making Selina laugh while she started the preparations for dinner. They were talking and laughing so much that Selina didn't hear the familiar rumble of Brody's motorbike arriving back, though Chad did, and redoubled his efforts to make her laugh. Nor did she hear the front door open, or Brody's footsteps as he entered the room. Not until he spoke did she realize he was present, and then she turned, her eyes going wide as saucers as he said;

"What the fucking hell is going on here?"

"Brody," Chad rose to his feet. "Hi."

Brody's smoldering gaze slid from Selina to his brother, and she gasped aloud at the look of pure dislike he leveled at the blond.

"Get out," Brody snapped coldly.

"Brody!" Selina said, shocked. "He's your *brother!*"

"*Half*-brother," Brody said harshly. "Get out of my house and stay away from my girlfriend. I don't wanna see your face around here again."

Distressed, Selina looked from one man to the other, unsure what to do. Chad held a hand out towards her placatingly.

"It's all right, Selina, I'll go. I wouldn't want to be the cause of any trouble between you two. It's been lovely to meet you, but as I suspected, you're far more than this ungrateful asshole deserves."

Brody started forward with a snarl at that, putting himself between Chad and Selina in a stance that she only later realized was clearly intended to be defensive of her. Chad only shrugged and left quietly.

Brody's broad shoulders didn't relax until the throaty rumble of the Porsche's engine had faded away into the distance. Finally he turned and looked down at Selina, frowning.

"Don't talk to him again, Selina."

"What the *hell* was all that about?" she demanded indignantly, ignoring his words, planting her hands on her hips and glaring up at him.

"Chad's not a good man..."

"Brody! Don't you dare be angry with me for trying to make your brother welcome when I didn't even know that you *had* a brother, never mind that you're obviously at odds with him!"

"Half-brother," he corrected again.

"He's still your *family*, Brody. For all I know, the only family you've got. I grew up in a succession of crappy foster-homes where I'd have given anything to have any family at all."

She was so beautiful with her hands on her slender hips like that, defiantly glaring up at him. Brody had to suppress a completely inappropriate urge to kiss her.

"He's an asshole, Selina. I cut him and his even bigger asshole of a father out of my life years ago." Turning away, he went to the fridge, grabbed out a beer. Uncapped it and took a long sip, gazing unseeing out of the window.

He felt a light touch at the small of his back after a moment, looked down to see Selina standing beside him, her eyes troubled as she looked up at him. "What about *your* father, Brody? Your mother?"

Screwing his eyes shut, he heaved a deep sigh before telling her the horrible truth. "My mother had an affair with Jason Marshall, Chad's father. Got pregnant by him. My dad was away with his ship — he was Navy — at the time. The day he arrived back, he got home to find a note telling him I was waiting to be picked up at the daycare... lying on top of divorce papers."

Selina's hand flew to her mouth in horror.

Brody nodded at her expression. "Yeah. I was four. Mom wanted nothing to do with me. Wanted to wipe me and Dad out of her past altogether. Only problem was... with Mom gone and me to look after, he got himself honorably discharged from the Navy and promptly fell to pieces. Drank himself to death. He died a couple of days before my eighth birthday."

"Oh God, Brody, I'm so sorry." Her big eyes brimmed with tears for him. "Did your mom take you back?"

"She didn't have much choice. Marshall was running for Congress, couldn't have an abandoned child spoiling the image of the perfect family. They'd paid Dad off to keep me, but with him dead — I was a dirty little secret she couldn't hide. She spun the story that Dad beat her and she'd fled for her life."

Selina's expression made him say "It wasn't true. She admitted as much to me before she died when I was sixteen."

Selina touched Brody's wrist gently, trying to caress away the tension in his hands, clenched white-knuckled on the edge of the counter. "Chad would have been just a kid then, though. He lost his mother too."

"He was a spoilt-rotten little shit," Brody said bitterly, "who I barely knew. I got packed off to boarding school aged ten and barely saw any of them for the next eight years, at which point the Congressman called me in and told me never to darken his doorstep again."

"Oh *Brody*."

"Don't grieve for me, angel. I was well rid of them. Got myself through college on an Army scholarship and found my spiritual home in the Rangers." He hesitated, turning to look out the window again. "It was a few years later when I ran across Chad again, quite by chance. I didn't even know who he was until I found out his name. But he knew me. He'd made it his mission to seduce my fiancée while I was away on deployment."

"You were *engaged*?" she gaped at him in utter shock. He'd certainly never mentioned *that* little fact!

"I was young and dumb. I thought she could wait for me. I was wrong." His mouth twisted cynically. "Now you see where my control-freak tendencies come from, Selina. It's not a pretty story, and it's why I'll never deal well with seeing Chad anywhere fucking *near* you."

"I won't let him near me again," she promised fervently, tucking herself under the arm he held out to her, pressing close to his side.

"Promise me," he whispered against her hair, his arm tightening around her.

"I promise," she rubbed her cheek on his shirt, breathing in the warm, masculine scent of him, before her hand came up and she plucked lightly at his belt buckle. "I'm here for you,

Brody. I'll always be here for you."

He sighed with pleasure as she unbuckled and unzipped, her small hand slipping into his pants and caressing lightly over his cock, which hardened swiftly under her touch. He gasped as she dropped to her knees, looking up at him from those beautiful doelike eyes which never failed to make him want her.

"Selina," he breathed, reaching to stroke her hair as her mouth opened and she licked lightly at the tip of his cock, just quick little flicks of her tongue at first, her hands moving to fondle his balls, stroke around the root of his cock. The last few weeks in Brody's bed had taught her exactly how to touch him to drive him utterly insane with lust, and she used every trick she'd learned to her advantage now.

"Christ," Brody had to lean one hand on the counter to keep himself upright as Selina suckled enthusiastically on his cock, stroking it with her hands too, humming happily in her throat, all the while keeping her eyes on his. "Oh God, baby, you're so good at that. So fucking good." He couldn't quite resist tightening his hands a little in her hair, rocking his hips to fuck into her mouth. She held still for it, just her tongue working, lapping at the underside of his cock.

Brody was careful not to push deep into Selina's mouth, since he knew she didn't like that. Not that he needed it. Just her warm wet lips around the tip, combined with the way she was looking up at him like that, was quite enough to drive him right out of his mind.

"Gotta fuck you," he panted suddenly, pulling her up to her feet to kiss her full, pouting lips thoroughly. "I gotta have you, Selina…"

She was already unbuttoning her blouse for him, sliding down the zip of her skirt, wriggling out of her clothes to leave her naked in his kitchen, holding out her arms in welcome. No man alive could have resisted such a temptation, and certainly not Brody Cullane.

The kitchen bench was the perfect height; he lifted her to it easily, spread her legs to look at her, at the glistening evidence of her arousal. She moaned as he tested her readiness with a probing finger, decided she needed a little more working up.

Bending Selina back over his arm, Brody bent his head to suckle at her breasts, at the pouting pink nipples he loved to tease, to pinch and bite. To clamp and tug on, see Selina sob with the pleasure/pain of the erotic touch. She cried out his name softly now, her fingers in his thick dark hair, as he used the edge of his teeth to give her what she needed, even as he thrust two thick fingers into her pussy, his thumb chafing roughly over her clit.

Selina threw her head back in wanton abandonment as Brody stimulated her, bringing her quickly to a state of desperation before pulling back and teasing lightly at her clit, licking softly at her nipple.

"Say it," he said between licks, "tell me what you want."

Her fingers clenched in his hair and she moaned with frustration. "You, Brody, I want you!"

"Tell me how."

"Hard!" she shouted, desperate. "Fuck me

good, do it rough, make me *yours!*"

"Yes," Brody growled deep in his throat, pulling Selina's hips to the edge of the counter, fitting his swollen, leaking cock to the soaked opening of her pussy. "You're *mine.*" And he drove home with one deep, powerful thrust of his hips.

Selina's ecstatic scream mingled with his possessive, triumphant snarl as he began to thrust, hard, strong hands clamped on her hips to keep her still, the powerful muscles of his thighs clenching as he sought to give her the deep, rough fucking he knew she loved best. Head flung back, lips parted with ecstasy as she writhed against him, she was the most beautiful thing he'd ever seen, and he gazed at her near-reverently as he slammed into her wet, willing body again and again.

It was rough, near-vicious, and Selina knew she'd have bruises on her hips later from the brutally strong grip of Brody's hands. Not that she cared; she always treasured the marks left on her skin from Brody's loving, felt that they were a visible, tangible reminder of his possession of her, body and soul.

She hadn't yet told him that she loved him; intuitively sensing that it would be a difficult thing for him to say to her, she hadn't wanted to put pressure on him to return the sentiment. But now, seeing his sudden insecurity, she couldn't hold back any longer with the words that she had been fighting to hold back for weeks now.

Pulling on his hair to bring his head close to hers for a deep, rough kiss, all tongue and teeth and Brody biting at her lower lip, when he pulled back she looked him straight in the eye and gasped out;

"I love you."

Brody's eyes widened; and then, for the first time since they'd begun sleeping together, he came first, with a strangled, shocked cry.

Feeling the flood of heat inside her, his cock jerking, his body tremoring uncontrollably for a moment, Selina held him close, raining kisses against his stubbled cheek as he groaned into her hair.

"Oh God, baby, I'm sorry, so sorry!" Brody was stricken with remorse as he eased out of Selina.

"It's okay, it's fine, darling," she shook her head at him.

"It's *not*." Hitching his pants up quickly, he scooped her easily up into his arms and carried her towards their bedroom. "That was terrible. A good Dom always sees to his sub's needs before his own."

She laughed at him gently, nestling happily into his arms. "As if I don't know that you'll make sure you *see to my needs* very thoroughly indeed, you silly man."

"I certainly will give you a good seeing to, and who are you calling silly?" He narrowed his eyes at her as he lowered her gently to the bed. "That, madam, deserves a punishment."

"Does it?" Selina fluttered her eyelashes. "Oh, no. Whatever will you do with me? I'm so *naughty*."

Brody had to laugh at Selina's mischievous expression as she sassed him. Leaning down to open the bottom drawer where he kept his (now expanded) collection of toys, he smirked back at her. "Well now. That's for me to know and you to find out." Lifting his hand, he showed her the blindfold and handcuffs dangling from it.

Selina chewed on her lower lip with anticipation as Brody clicked a cuff onto one of her wrists, checking to be sure it wasn't too tight. It was thickly padded, but she had a tendency to yank hard when he had her really worked up and he didn't want her getting loose.

"Over here, angel," he urged her to turn over, and then looped the handcuff chain around the thick corner bedpost before clicking the other cuff on. "Now this. Comfy?"

"Yes," Selina whispered, throat tight with excitement, as he eased the blindfold over her eyes.

"Good," Brody said quietly. "On your feet."

She stood beside the bed, bent over slightly with the handcuffs pulling on her wrists, listening as she waited in silence. He was removing his own clothes, she could tell from the faint sounds as he moved around, and soon she felt him step past her and sit down on the bed.

"So pretty," Brody murmured, looking at Selina, chained to his bed and waiting eagerly to be punished. There was a beautiful flush of arousal all the way from her pretty breasts to her hairline, her soft pink lips parted as she breathed fast. "Looking forward to teaching you a lesson, naughty girl."

"Yes, sir," Selina whimpered as he reached out to fondle her breasts, pinching and twisting her nipples until they ached. "Oh God, yes sir, please, teach me how to be a good girl. I want to be a good girl for you."

"Do you, indeed? I think you're very *bad*. And bad girls get punished." Cool metal touched her skin, and Selina sucked in a sharp breath as he carefully adjusted the nipple clamps to the perfect tension, just enough pain to make her knees shake and her breath slip into the slow, deep breaths of subspace, endorphins flooding her system.

They almost never needed to use safe words any more, though Selina was aware, in the back of her mind, that Brody would respect her request instantly if she did. She relaxed into his touch now, going almost limp as he pulled her over his knee, sitting back so her forehead and breasts rested on the mattress while her feet remained on the floor.

"Beautiful," Brody murmured, smoothing the palm of his hand over Selina's smoothly rounded buttocks. "Just beautiful."

She whined in response, wiggling — he realized she was deliberately rubbing her clamped nipples on the mattress, trying to get more friction.

"Bad, wicked girl," he dealt the first slap to her ass, savoring the low, frantic moan she let out. "Such a *dirty* girl." His fingers slipped between her legs, delving into her cleft, dripping with his seed. "Absolutely *filthy*."

Selina panted with need as a wet finger pressed between her ass cheeks for a moment, rimming her puckered little hole. She tried to squirm back onto Brody's finger — which promptly led to another spank.

"You really are being a bad girl today, aren't you, sweetheart?" Brody crooned, stroking the reddened mark on her bottom. "Dear me. This calls for something *special* in the way of punishment, I think." He'd stealthily laid out several toys on the mattress before pulling Selina onto his lap, reached out to select one now, a new one he'd bought specially for her a few days ago and hadn't had the chance to try out yet. "This one, I think. Hold still now."

Selina panted, fingers clawing at the wooden bedpost as she tried to obey Brody's command, but he was sliding something big inside her, something that didn't feel like the dildo he'd sometimes used on her. Something bigger. A second pressure at her ass made her suck in a sharp breath against the mattress.

Brody grinned as he watched Selina take the double vibrator, moaning and shaking as he pushed it deep. It had another surprise for her, though, as she discovered when he finally had it nestled all the way inside her and switched it on.

Two little silicone rabbit ears began to twitch and vibrate, driving her mad, her wrists jerking helplessly against the restraints, frantic moans and cries escaping her lips as she writhed and thrashed.

"Oh, no you don't," he held her still with a firm hand on the small of her back, the other holding the vibrator firmly in place. "I told you to be still."

"C-can't, Brody, Brody, *please!*" she sobbed out finally. Lifting his hand from her back, he brought it down on her bottom in another firm smack. And another, and a third, continuing until her bottom was bright red and she was screaming in orgasmic pleasure, twisting and writhing, her feet kicking in the air as she lay across his lap.

Gently, Brody eased Selina off his lap and down to the mattress, where she lay, gasping for breath. He soon had the handcuffs removed, but he didn't take the vibrator out just yet, just switching it off for a little while to let her recover. Removing one of her nipple clamps, he lay beside her, drawing her red, swollen nipple into his mouth and nursing it with his tongue in slow, gentle swirls. She brought a hand down, caressed his hair and the back of his neck, sighing with pleasure at his tender attentions. After a little while she reached her other hand to draw her blindfold off, looking down at his bent head, the expression of pleasure on his face as he suckled on her breast.

"The other one, please," she whispered, and he was quick to oblige, though couldn't resist just teasing her nipple with the tip of his tongue before releasing the clamp and drawing it into his mouth, laving it gently with his hot, wet tongue.

Selina moaned and shivered, each gentle draw of Brody's mouth against her nipples felt directly connected to the still-ongoing tremors in her pussy; she could feel the vibrator still deep inside her though it was switched off, guessed Brody hadn't finished with her yet.

She was proved right a little later as his hand stealthily crept back between her thighs to switch the vibrator back on, at a low setting at first.

Selina shifted and sighed as Brody's hand

began to move the vibrator about inside her, searching for her most sensitive spots, the rabbit ears just brushing her swollen clit lightly every now and again.

"That's it," Brody whispered, watching her eyelids flutter, her breathing quicken again. "That's it, Selina, feels good, doesn't it, angel? You gonna come for me again?"

She whimpered, fingernails digging into his broad shoulders as she strained to get more stimulation. He had no intention of making this one quick and easy for her, though; kept just teasing the rabbit ears around her clit, knowing the vibrator was running at too low a speed to get her off.

Brody could have lain there pleasuring Selina for hours, just watching her face, delighting in her ecstasy. She was utterly beautiful to him like this; though she was a pretty girl it was a quiet, unflashy sort of beauty, not the kind to stop traffic. To Brody, though, Selina in the throes of passion was the most beautiful sight he'd ever witnessed. The thought that he might lose her was suddenly a choking terror in his throat.

What if she preferred Chad to Brody? Chad was, after all, five years younger, handsome, rich — he liked to spoil his girlfriends, Brody knew only too well. Selina would be pampered and cared for, treated like a princess. Until Chad got bored with her, at least. *If* he got bored with her. Brody couldn't imagine *ever* being bored of Selina, of her passion, her laughter, her sass, the way she looked at him from those soft dark eyes and moaned his name in her throaty voice...

She was moaning his name again now, and

Brody suddenly realized she was close to orgasm again.

"Come on, angel," he encouraged her, turning the vibrator up a little faster. "You can get there. Come on, let me see you... oh God, you're so beautiful like this."

It was a particularly intense orgasm that ripped through her, he could tell, watching her body writhe, listening to the pitch of her wild screams. He turned the vibrator down to a dull buzz, easing her down gently, before switching it off and removing it entirely.

Selina sighed with lingering pleasure as Brody drew her into his arms, holding her close, her head nestled on his broad chest. He said nothing, just stroked her hair and her back slowly, holding her close until her breathing and pulse eased back to normal.

"You okay, angel?" he whispered finally.

"Mm," she roused herself from her semi-somnolent drowse to lean up on one elbow, smile down at him. "So much better than just *okay.*"

Brody smiled, smoothing a stray wisp of hair back behind her ear. "Good. I was a little rough on you."

She shook her head in disagreement; he reached down and patted her ass in response, making her wince.

"Yes, Selina, I was rough. I'm sorry."

"Brody, I loved every minute of it." Shifting slightly, she leaned further over him to kiss him. "Don't you dare apologize for doing something that made me feel so amazingly good."

He smiled slightly at that, returned to gently

stroking his fingers down her spine. Selina rested her head back on his chest, listening to the slow, steady *thump* of his heartbeat. Lay there for several long minutes relaxing before her eyes suddenly flew wide open.

"Oh, damn, I forgot to put dinner in the oven!"

Brody laughed, pulling her back down as she tried to scramble off the bed. "Too late now, angel. Forget it. We'll get takeout."

She sighed and rolled her eyes before settling down back into bed beside him, tracing her fingertips lightly over his defined abdominal muscles. It was a long time before either of them spoke again, and then it was Selina, in a very quiet voice.

"Why did Chad come here?"

Brody heaved a sigh. "I've been wondering that myself, angel."

"He knew my name."

"Did he now?" Brody's body tensed. "That's... worrying."

She petted his stomach lightly, trying to get him to relax. He hugged her a little tighter before letting out an explosive breath. "I guess you've met a lot of folks around here. And even though he's in a different branch of the forces, it wouldn't be all that hard to keep tabs on me. Not with his kind of money."

"Money?" Selina queried.

"His father was an old-money Republican congressman, Selina, who spent his time in office feathering his nest even further. Left Chad the lot when he died a few years ago."

"Why's he still in the military, then?" Selina

asked curiously. "If he's that rich? He was telling me how much he loves flying..."

Brody's laugh was bitter. "Did he have you believing he's a fighter pilot, then? He's not. He flies Air Force VIP jets, basically using the job as an opportunity to kiss as much ass as humanly possible, hoping to get enough influence and favors to make himself electable."

Selina's face screwed up in disgust.

"That's exactly what I think. But trust me, nobody anywhere is ever gonna elect him. I don't have enough dirt on him to get him drummed out of the Air Force, not with his connections, but there are a *lot* of people he's screwed over who will appear out of the woodwork if he ever tries to run for public office." A small smile of satisfaction played around his lips at the thought before he turned serious again. "His father was an asshole, but Chad's a real nasty piece of work, baby. Promise me you'll be careful? If anything happened to you — I couldn't bear it if anything happened to you, and he's bastard enough to come after you to get to me. He already proved that once."

Selina held him tightly as he buried his face in her hair. "Will you tell me about her?" she asked quietly after a little while.

"Who?"

"Your fiancée. The one who slept with Chad."

"Tiana?" He was still quite relaxed against her, which surprised Selina. She'd thought he would have tensed up again. "There's not much to tell, baby. It was so long ago. I was twenty-seven, she was twenty-three. I spent a lot of time in hot ugly sandy places in the early part of the last decade. I was stupid to think she could wait; she was a needy sub. Taught me a lesson about getting attached."

There wasn't much Selina could say to that, but "And Chad seduced her?"

"From what I could piece together, I hadn't been gone more than a couple of weeks before he made a move. He kept stringing her along until I got back, convinced her to break it off with me very publicly, and then promptly dumped her. She came crawling back to me, I said I wasn't up for taking back a woman who'd been sleeping with my stepbrother for months, and I haven't seen her since." There was no anger in his voice towards Tiana, Selina thought, and said as much.

"I'm not angry at her, not now. I was at the time, but I suspect Chad completely swept her off her feet, with money and attention. Flattered her and showered her with gifts and was generally there to be the Dom she needed." Brody shrugged. "I hope she found someone who was good to her. She deserved better than to be caught up in our family mess."

Selina stroked his stomach lightly again while she thought about what she wanted to say next. "Why does he hate you so much?" she asked finally.

"Good question; I've no idea. Chad was the golden boy, I was very much the outsider, the unwanted child they had no choice to take in after Dad died. I look very much like my father; my mother didn't want to lay eyes on me and my stepfather despised me."

"How could *anyone* do that to their own

child?" Selina burst out when Brody seemed unfazed by it. "I mean, I grew up in foster homes which were — well, not fantastic — but I used to *dream* of having family of my own. Someone to love me just because I was part of their family, you know?"

Brody smiled sadly down at her. "Well, I guess I'm living proof that not all families are happy, baby. It doesn't matter, it's long since water under the bridge. They're all dead now except Chad, and frankly I'm quite happy to pretend he is too. It's really worrying me that he turned up here today and knew your name, though. Promise me you'll be careful?"

She could see the concern, the caring, in his eyes. Reached up to kiss him, hold onto him tightly.

"I promise."

Selina was quite sure she would have no trouble keeping her promise to Brody. She'd seen the brief flicker of fear in Chad's eyes when confronted with Brody's anger and was sure he wouldn't risk coming by the house again. But she hadn't understood the depths of his cunning, she realized when she looked up one morning at work and found him smiling down at her, dressed in an expensive-looking three-piece suit instead of his Air Force uniform.

"Hi, Selina."

"What are you doing here?" she said coolly.

He did his best to look guileless. "I need an appointment. This *is* a doctor's office."

"A civilian doctor. I suggest you see a doctor on base." She looked back down at the stack of printed prescriptions she was sorting, willing her fingers not to shake.

"Well, I don't necessarily want to see a military doctor," he leaned forward, spoke in a confidential tone.

"Why, is it an STD?" she said loudly, making the entire waiting room look up in shock and Chad flinch back. His face darkened for a moment.

"I see Brody's been filling your ears with lies about me," he said, in an admirably even tone, considering the insult she'd just thrown. "I'll be the bigger man, then, and not tell you about the hell he put our mother through. About how I was hoping you'd be an intermediary for us to actually become a family. He's the only family I've got, Selina. I don't want to spend the rest of my life at odds with him because of a stupid mistake I made years ago."

"Seducing his fiancée was a *mistake*?" she said coldly, though inwardly she began to wonder. *Family...* she knew all too well the longing for a true family. Chad was just as alone as she was.

"I was twenty-two and I fell in love," he spread his hands helplessly. "I had no idea Tiana was involved with Brody — that she even *knew* Brody! — until he came back from deployment and she left me and went running back to him."

"I don't believe you," Selina said, but her tone lacked conviction, and Chad sensed it. He didn't press the advantage, though, just giving her a sad smile.

"I won't push, Selina. Just, be careful with Brody. He's got a long history of being an asshole to women. Just like his father." Reaching out, he touched a light fingertip to a faint bruise on her wrist, giving her a knowing look. "I suspect he's not as careful with you as he should be."

And with that parting shot, he turned on his heel and walked out, leaving Selina with a miserably confused stew of emotions churning in her stomach. She put her head in her hands and took a few deep breaths.

"I don't think I'd trust that one, dearie," she looked up in surprise as an old lady sitting near the reception desk spoke. The old lady's friend, sitting beside her, nodded vigorously in agreement.

"Never trust a pretty face," she said sagely. "All looks and no substance."

"Sounded just like a politician," the first old lady agreed, which made Selina twitch. Chad's father was a Republican congressman, she remembered. *He probably learned to lie at his father's knee.*

The intercom on the desk buzzed, and she forced a smile and rose to her feet. "Dr Cassite is ready to see you now, Mrs Brown."

"You're quiet tonight," Brody said that evening after dinner, as Selina curled up next to him on the couch. "Something bothering you, baby?"

She hesitated before looking up at him. "Can I ask you something?"

"Anything, you know that." He tilted his head at her curiously, took her hand in his to stroke her fingers lightly.

Taking a deep breath, she asked "Could we try

some more... *vanilla* sex?"

Startled, Brody stared at her for a moment before saying "Of course we can, baby!" Immediately, though, he started to feel guilty; wondered if Selina was trying to tell him that he was too rough with her in bed. Covering his sudden concern with a smile, he reached his arm around her, pulled her into his lap. "It's all for your pleasure, you know that. Some slow sweet lovemaking sounds delightful."

Slim arms winding around his neck, she smiled at him. "Slow and sweet sounds *perfect*. Shall we go to bed, then?"

"Why?" he grinned. "We could start here. Just some kissing, maybe. A little bit of touching..." Like being a teenager again, he thought, necking with a pretty girl. Not that Selina was all that far out of her teens herself. She smiled again at his remark before leaning in to kiss him. All too soon she pulled back, though.

"Will you be able to get off, though, Brody?"

He had to laugh. "Sweetheart, what gets me off is seeing *you* enjoying yourself. You already know it doesn't take much to get me hard for you." Deliberately, he shifted his hips, grinding his groin up against her, showing her wordlessly that he had no problems at all in that department.

Selina gasped — and then rocked her hips back against him, running her fingers into his hair, holding on tightly as she pressed her lips against his, tongue flickering lightly between them.

Amused by her apparent desire to take the initiative — and not a little aroused — Brody was more than happy to go along; just making out with her was a perfectly delightful experience anyway. Soon enough she was impatiently pulling her shirt over her head and grabbing his hands to bring them to her breasts; he cautioned himself firmly to be gentle and satisfied himself with just playing with her nipples lightly, teasing and rolling them slowly between finger and thumb.

Selina ached for more, though, and Brody wasn't obliging her. Reaching down between them she groped for his belt buckle, pulled it open and unbuttoned his pants.

"Mm," Brody murmured, "that the way it's gonna be, huh? You wanna ride my cock, sweetheart?"

"Yes," while she'd been on his lap before, it had only been facing away from him, Brody still keeping the initiative. Sitting astride his thighs, Selina thought that she'd quite like to try it the other way about.

"Let's get the rest of these clothes off then, hmm? Don't deny me the sight of you naked in my lap."

She smiled at that, stood to strip off the rest of her clothes even as he quickly wriggled out of his, and then returned quickly to his waiting arms.

"Stand up here," Brody suggested, patting the couch on either side of his thighs. "Let me get you wet."

"Already wet," she admitted with a giggle, but then riding his face sounded nearly as good as riding his cock, and he most definitely knew what to do with his tongue. She ended up with a knee on the back of the couch, her hands braced on the wall and both Brody's hands on her ass as he buried his face in her pussy, licking through the delicate folds slowly, his eyes on hers.

"More," she demanded, grabbing his head and pushing it against her; felt him smile before he obeyed, lapping harder at her clit and then pursing his lips and suckling on it.

Selina's lips parted, her breath hissing out between them in soft pants as Brody worked her over with his tongue and lips until she pulled back abruptly. He looked up at her quizzically, lips and chin shining with her slick, wondering why she'd stopped him. Normally she loved it when he brought her to climax with his mouth. She was in a really strange mood today, he thought again; not that he was objecting as she sank down, settling her knees on either side of his hips and wrapping a slim hand around his straining, swollen cock to guide it up into her sopping channel.

"Yeahhh," Brody groaned with pleasure as Selina sank slowly down on him, withdrawing her hand from between them as she took him in deep. "That's it, baby, ride me, take what you want."

It felt good, it felt really good, Brody's thick, hard cock buried deep inside her as she pushed down, taking him all the way inside her until she was seated on his thighs. Settling her hands on his broad shoulders to stabilize herself, Selina began to rock, gasping with pleasure as the tip of his arousal rubbed over her G-spot.

It was good — but it wasn't what she usually got with Brody, it wasn't the amazing, all-encompassing passion that consumed her so utterly she was left a drained, gasping wreck in his arms. It took Brody sliding a hand down between them to play with her clit while his other hand wreaked havoc on her nipples before she could come, and she strongly suspected that Brody had been fighting to hold back his own climax just to make sure that she did.

Lying against his chest afterwards, she heaved a sigh.

"That does not sound like happiness to be here," Brody said quietly, smoothing her hair back from her face. "Didn't you enjoy that, angel?"

"I did, it was great!" but even to her own ears, her voice held a falsely bright quality.

Brody said nothing. Just stroked her hair until finally, Selina sighed again. "I'm sorry, Brody."

"What for?" he sounded genuinely surprised.

"It wasn't as good, and I know it's not what you like..."

"Shh," he tilted her chin up, smiled at her lovingly. "Selina, sweetheart — any way I get to touch you is perfect to me. No matter what it is that you want, or think that you want, I am more than happy to give it to you."

"I'm pretty sure you know what it is that I want a lot better than I do," she muttered, suddenly seeing the funny side and starting to chuckle.

"That's kind of the whole point of me being your Dom, angel," he grinned at her, though he was still in the dark as to why she'd wanted to try more 'vanilla' sex in the first place. He tried to ask, but she only shook her head, pressing her face against his neck.

"It doesn't matter, Brody. I was being silly."

"Selina..."

She grabbed his face in her hands and kissed him fiercely, pulling back to fix him with a pleading stare. "Take me to bed, Brody. Please. You know what I need."

He held her gaze for a long moment before nodding. "All right." Dropping into his Dom voice, he said sternly "But you're going to do *exactly* as you're told, all right?"

Selina nodded submissively as he stood, scooping her easily up in his arms. "Yes, Brody."

"Yes, what?" he narrowed his eyes at her.

"Yes, Sir," she gave the right answer this time, smiling up at him happily as he carried her to their bedroom.

When a month went by without Chad turning up again, Selina began to feel that he'd probably given up. She mentioned him to Brody once or twice; each time Brody only shrugged and said;

"Like the proverbial bad penny, he'll turn up some time. Stay away, Selina. He's bad news."

"I can't imagine he'll risk it, can you?" she said. "He knows you have it in for him, and I accused him of having an STD in front of a whole crowd of people."

Brody had roared with laughter when she finally told him the story and praised her to the skies. He grinned again at the memory before sobering. "Still. I wouldn't trust him within an inch of you, baby. If he turns up again, I'll get a damn restraining order."

Comforted by that thought, Selina forgot

about Chad and relaxed back into her routine. Brody still hadn't told her that he loved her, but, understanding more now about his history with women, she didn't push for it. He showed her how much he cared anyway, with his thoughtfulness and consideration, always putting her wants and needs above his own, frequently bringing her unexpected gifts of flowers or chocolate, showing his clear pride that she was with him when they went out together.

She realized how wrong she'd been to forget about Chad one day when she arrived home to find his Porsche in the driveway again. She debated turning her bike around and riding away again, but it had just started to rain lightly and she wasn't wearing a coat.

"Damned if I'll let him drive me away from my home," her natural stubbornness came to the fore, and she dismounted the bike, pushing it up the driveway and into the garage. Chad was sitting on the porch seat, watching her.

"You can go now," she said coolly, mounting the steps and fishing her key out of her bag. "I really don't think you want to be here when Brody gets home."

She honestly hadn't been expecting his next move; when he got up and crowded her against the door as she unlocked it, forcing it open and her inside, she turned on him, startled.

"What the fuck d'you think you're doing?"

"Selina, I know Brody's not taking good care of you. Making you go out to work, for God's sake, riding around on a push bike instead of buying you a car." He closed the door behind them and looked down at her, reaching out to lightly touch her neck and the hickey Brody had left there the previous evening. "Leaving bruises on you where anyone can see."

Furious, she slapped his hand away. "Don't you dare touch me! Brody's not *making* me do anything. I work because I like working, I like to keep busy. And I'd buy myself a damn car if I wanted one."

Chad shook his head at her condescendingly, and she realized he literally hadn't listened to a word she'd said. "You deserve so much better. A beautiful girl like you, you deserve to be treasured and pampered, kept in style. Designer clothes to wear, beautiful jewelry..." he put a hand in his jacket pocket, pulled out a long, slim box. "This is for you, Selina."

"Are you serious?" she said disbelievingly.

"Of course." He opened the box and smirked at her smugly. "It'll look magnificent on you."

She looked down into the box by instinct as he thrust it under her nose; what she saw there had her recoiling, because it was no ordinary piece of jewelry. The triple strand of pearls were beautiful, creamy, large and perfectly matched — and they were clearly intended to be a *collar*. There was even a thick gold D-ring in the front.

"You disgusting piece of pond-sucking *scum*," she said, clearly and distinctly, looking up at him.

"I beg your pardon!" Chad's face darkened with rage. "You can't speak to me like that, you little slut!"

"I can say anything I fucking well want, you asshole, because you just pushed your way into *my home* and propositioned me in the most disgustingly insulting manner *possible*." Selina's blood was up, but she didn't shout or rage. She said every word with icily clear precision, her fury at his insulting, entitled attitude nakedly apparent on her face. "Brody is worth a *thousand* of you. He loves me, even if he's not too good at saying it because of the trust issues he has with women — because of the disgusting trick *you* played with his fiancée. I'm staying. There's absolutely nothing you could offer me that would *even for one moment* tempt me to let you lay a *single finger* on me."

Chad for a moment seemed utterly lost for words, startled by her rage. Emboldened by having shut down his smooth patter, Selina pushed out her hand, shoving the box and its unwanted contents away from her. "So you can take that piece of filth and shove it where the sun don't shine!"

She'd pushed him over the edge, she saw it instantly as his expression changed from shock to thwarted lust, and she took three hasty steps backwards, grabbing for the drawer in the hall table even as Chad reached to try and grab her.

He froze as she brought the barrel of the pistol up to level it at his face.

"You wouldn't dare," he said.

"Try me." Her eyes were absolutely steady as she stared at him over the gun. "Brody taught me how to use this after you turned up the first time. I thought he was being paranoid. Seems I was wrong."

He seemed to be considering whether to try and wrest the gun from her when the door behind him opened quietly and Brody stepped inside.

"She's become quite a shot, Chad. I wouldn't test her willingness to pull the trigger if I were you," he said evenly.

Relieved beyond measure to see him, Selina let the gun barrel drop. Chad lunged for it in the same instant — but Brody had been fully prepared for that. Far better trained in hand-to-hand combat than his younger brother, he moved so quickly he was almost a blur.

It was almost too fast for Selina to see. Bemused, she just stared as Chad crashed to the floor in front of her, Brody astride his back, efficiently wrenching an arm up behind his back until Chad screamed.

"You ever come near Selina again," Brody said in a near-conversational tone, "and I'll just let her goddamn well shoot you."

"Let go..." Chad's furious demand trailed off in another scream as Brody wrenched a little harder.

"All right, sir, we'll take it from here," another voice said, and Selina looked up, startled, as two uniformed military police officers entered through the open front door. One of them, a woman, stepped briskly forward and took the gun gently from Selina's nerveless fingers with a reassuring smile.

"You won't be needing that, miss. It's all right, you're quite safe now."

She blinked, startled. "Why — why are you here? Why is Brody here?" she asked, her voice a little thin, and the female MP cast a quick glance at where Brody was capably assisting her partner to cuff Chad, wrapped a comforting arm around Selina's shoulders and guided her into the lounge.

"Lieutenant Colonel Cullane came to us a few weeks ago with his concerns," the MP gently eased Selina down to sit on the couch. "We've had Captain Marshall under surveillance for some time. Catching him in the act of forcing his way in here and attempting to assault you was the cherry on top of our case against him, frankly."

Selina put her head in her hands. She was beginning to shake with reaction, didn't really understand what was being said. A few moments later she heard Brody's voice, felt the woman beside her get up, and then Brody was taking her place, a solid, comforting presence as he put his arms around Selina and hugged her close. Too stunned — and still too angry — for tears, she rested her head against the strong curve of his neck and just breathed in his warm, masculine scent for a few minutes, letting his quiet strength soothe her.

"What's going on?" she felt strong enough to ask finally. The house had fallen quiet some minutes before, the MPs obviously having taken Chad away. "That officer said you went to her weeks ago. Why?"

Brody sighed. "I didn't tell you because I didn't want to worry you. After you admitted that he turned up to hassle you at work, I decided to do a little bit of checking up. Got a friend to enable a tracking chip in Chad's phone. We looked at the data after a couple of days, and, Selina... he was *stalking* you. Every time you left the house, or left work, he was loitering somewhere nearby watching you."

"Oh my God," she began to shake again, and Brody hauled her into his lap, rubbed her back, told her to breathe slowly.

"I went to the MPs then, but they told me there was nothing they could do without evidence. Even though they already had a person of interest file open on him, there was absolutely nothing they could pin on him. I did convince them to start tailing you when you were on your way to or from work, since that would be the most likely time for him to try something — and it seems I was right. You were never in danger, honey. Even if you hadn't gotten to the gun first — though I'm very proud that you did, and that you faced him down like that — we were right outside the door the whole time. I heard everything you said to him, you brave, wonderful, *amazing* girl."

She smiled at that, hid her face against his shoulder. "I was too mad at what an arrogant asshat he was being to be frightened at the time," she admitted. "But now I think about it — what would he have done to me, Brody?"

"Shh," he pressed his face against her hair. "Don't think about it, angel. Just don't." His voice was a little hoarse, but he did his best to keep it steady for her sake. He could feel Selina's slight body shaking in his arms as she tried, he suspected, to hold back sobs. "It's all right," he said soothingly against her hair, tightening his arms around her. "It's all right to cry, sweetheart, I'm here for you."

She let it out then, gasping breaths and deep, husking sobs, soaking his shirt with her tears while he rocked her and crooned soothingly, his arms firm around her, reassuring her that he was there, that he would *always* be there for her.

"I love you," he whispered against her hair just as she was finally quieting, which promptly set her off again and made him smile ruefully. "That's pretty much what I deserve for being an emotionally constipated asshole who struggles to find the words to tell you how much you mean to me, huh? Well I'm tellin' you now. I nearly died when I thought he was gonna hurt you. Couldn't bear it if anything happened to you, my darling."

Her sobs were quieter now as she listened, as Brody kept talking, the words pouring out of him in a great rush. He told her how she'd crept into his heart with her sassy ways and her cheeky looks, the way she was only a submissive in the bedroom.

Selina laughed weakly against his neck at that. "God, would Chad ever have been in for a nasty shock if I'd accepted his offer!"

Brody hugged her tighter, thinking privately that Chad would have beaten the shit out of Selina for daring to talk back to him. He would never tell her that, though, saying instead; "He certainly would. A sassy sub ain't his style at all. Didn't used to think it was mine, either — not until you."

She laughed at that, pulled back to look at him. Even with red-rimmed eyes and tear-tracks on her cheeks, Brody thought she was still one of the most beautiful women he'd ever laid eyes on.

His hand was still in her hair, he tightened it

slightly, pulling her towards him a little, before stopping to wait, the action a silent question.

Selina smiled and leaned in the rest of the way to kiss him, her lips soft and tremulous against his.

Brody's possessive streak roared to the fore; he'd been keeping it suppressed by sheer effort of will ever since he entered the house to find Selina holding Chad at bay with a gun as Chad tried to put a damned collar on her. On *Brody's* girl, *his* Selina.

"*Mine*," he growled against her mouth, rejoiced in Selina's answering moan of acquiescence. She tugged at his shirt, trying to undo the buttons; he pulled back long enough to strip it off swiftly before reaching back for her. She'd already tugged her own shirt off over her head and he smiled hungrily to see the pretty turquoise-blue bra he'd bought for her when they went shopping the previous week.

"That looks glorious against your skin," he murmured, "but even better off, I'll bet."

She laughed and unfastened the bra, tossing it aside and deliberately putting her hands back behind her back, thrusting out her breasts. "What do you think?"

He gave the only answer he possibly could, pushing her down on the couch, one arm snaking behind her to hold her wrists at the small of her back while his other hand and mouth worshiped her breasts. Her skirt rose up to her hips as she wrapped her legs around his waist, rocking her groin against his thickening erection.

"So wet," Brody groaned against her breast,

his hand moving down to edge her panties aside, thick fingers rubbing over slick, sensitive flesh. "So wet for me, baby."

"All for you," deliberately she struggled a little against his firm hold on her wrists, making him growl possessively and bite down on her nipple. He heard her breathing hitch and then slow, smiled to himself.

"Ready to submit to me yet, angel?" he laved the bite with his tongue gently.

"Yes," Selina whispered, feeling the first flood of heat wash through her as Brody's fingers pressed deeper into her pussy. "I'm yours, Brody."

"Yes you are." Pulling back and standing up, he unfastened his belt, pulled it from the waist loops of his pants with a thoughtful look. "Turn over."

She obeyed instantly; he no longer needed to resort to his Dom voice to command her in intimate situations. Selina's trust in him was complete; he knew what she needed, far better than she did. She moaned in delight as the thick, tough leather wrapped efficiently around her wrists, securing her hands at the small of her back. Brody checked the restraint with a tug before he unbuttoned her skirt and smoothed it down off her hips, taking her panties down with it, leaving her nude on her knees on the couch.

"So lovely," he murmured, warm hand on the back of her neck pressing her down to lean over the arm of the couch, ass in the air for him. "You good there, baby?"

"Yes, oh yes," she panted, spreading her knees and steadying herself. "Please, Brody!"

He made her wait while he took his boots off, removed his pants, watching her shift and plead, rubbing her breasts against the fabric of the couch, trying for stimulation.

"Naughty, needy girl," the first spank on her bottom made Selina jump; she hadn't been expecting it. His hand on her back steadied her before the second one came, a blissfully firm swat that made her close her eyes and relax into it. She made a low, hungry sound in her throat, rolling her hips invitingly.

"Please, Brody. I want you in me, want you to fuck me. Fill me up," she gasped out the words in between spanks. "Please, sir. I'll be so good for you."

"You're always good for me." Brody couldn't resist any longer, had to have her. His cock was throbbing, achingly erect. Sitting down on the couch, he turned her around and pulled her down on his lap, facing him; she gasped as the reddened skin of her abused ass landed hard on his thighs.

"Green?" he checked, brushing her hair out of her face.

"Definitely green," Selina gasped, rubbing her soaked pussy against his erection, desperate to get him inside her.

"Good." His hands curved around her hips to lift her; he positioned himself carefully and then drove home with one deep thrust, watching as Selina's eyes rolled back in her head, her lips parting on a scream of ecstasy. "That's it. That's it, good girl, oh my beautiful angel..." he set up a pounding, fast rhythm, slamming up into Selina, one of his hands going behind her to catch her bound wrists, pull lightly to arch her back, push her breasts up towards his face. She sobbed with pleasure, going limp, letting him manhandle her as he wished — except her internal muscles were already beginning to suck at him, a tight wet ripple tugging on his cock as her climax overwhelmed her.

"Selina!" he shouted her name as her clenching pussy sucked his own orgasm right out of him, leaving him shaking and gasping with the sudden intensity of it, the ripple of pleasure down his spine going on and on for long, blissful moments as Selina's body tremored around him.

At last he felt her go limp again, let go of the belt around her wrists so she could fall forward and lean her forehead on his shoulder. Gently, knowing how much she loved to be held after lovemaking, he unwound the belt and released her hands, pulling her close and holding her head against the crook of his neck as he stroked her hair and hummed a soft, soothing melody to her.

"I love you," Selina whispered against his throat after a few long, heavenly minutes of cuddling, and Brody smiled. Now was the time to say it back, he realized; he'd already said it to her and meant it, so now it should be easy.

But when he opened his mouth, the words that came out instead were "Will you marry me?"

Selina startled back, looked at Brody wide-eyed. He looked almost as surprised as she felt, so she asked hesitantly;

"Do you mean that?"

"Hell yeah!" Brody answered immediately, realizing it was totally true. Selina as his wife was the best future he could ever imagine. Maybe even kids, one day, if she felt that was something they could do. Bright-eyed little moppets with her sass and love of life. The more he thought about it, the more he loved the idea. A *family*, the first true family either he or Selina had ever had, and the only one he could ever imagine wanting. Putting his hand to her cheek gently, he told her earnestly;

"I love you more than I know how to say and I can't imagine my life without you in it. Please say you'll marry me?"

Selina smiled through the happy tears beginning to well in her eyes. "Yes. Of course I'll marry you, Brody Cullane." She leaned in for a kiss, and he hugged her tightly.

"I promise you'll never regret it," he told her.

"I know," was all she said, smiling back at him starry-eyed, snuggling into his arms. Utterly content to be in the one place in the world she knew, beyond doubt, she would always get exactly what she needed.

~ THE END ~

CAITLYN LYNCH

Turn the page to read my FREE bonus novella,
Hot For Heather!

Hot For Heather

Closing the piano lid, Heather dropped her head to rest her heated brow against the cool wooden surface. She was too hot, too frustrated to play any more today. The AC was on the blink, had been for days, and the hundred-degree weather outside had her nerves fraying and her fingers slipping on the ivory keys, making uncharacteristic mistakes in her usually expert playing.

Getting up, she headed into the kitchen, opened the refrigerator to grab a soda and sighed in all-too-brief relief as the chill air washed over her. Her nipples perked up with interest, pressing against the thin shirt that was all she was wearing, and she sighed.

"No action today, I'm afraid."

Nor in quite some time. Maybe that's why I can't get any passion into my music lately... even the symphony director had noticed it, had told her crudely to go out and get laid, even while unsubtly hinting that he'd be quite happy to help her out. Heather suppressed a shudder of distaste at the memory.

She closed the refrigerator reluctantly and turned away, cracking the soda to take a long, thirsty gulp before drifting over to the window, lifting the curtain to peer out into the bright daylight.

The view that greeted her was unexpected but not unwelcome; a shirtless, heavily muscled man lifting a large box from the trunk of a car and turning to walk up the steps into her building. His eyes met hers as she stared at him through the window and he nodded in greeting.

Startled, Heather let the curtain drop, backed away. Irresolute for a moment, she quickly made up her mind and headed for her apartment door. The guy must be delivering something, and if it was for Mrs Flanagan upstairs, the old lady was completely deaf and wouldn't hear the bell.

Opening the door, she made to turn right towards the front door and bounced straight off the large cardboard box held by the even larger male who was already coming in.

Heather lost her balance and ended up sitting on the floor, legs splayed in a very undignified manner, looking up at the offending cardboard box in affront.

"Watch yourself there," a deep voice drawled, and she looked up past the box to find brown eyes twinkling down at her from a tanned face with the most beautifully chiselled cheekbones, shown off to perfection by a very short haircut and a clean-shaven, square-cut jaw.

"What are you doing?" was all she could squeak out as he shouldered open the door to the apartment opposite hers and went in.

"Moving in," came the cheerful response, before he came back out, arms empty, and looked down at her still sitting on the floor. "Did I hurt ya?" He offered a large, squarish hand to help her up.

"No-no, I'm fine," she accepted the hand and let him help her up. "You can't be moving in, though. That apartment belongs to Mrs Flanagan's grandson, he's on deployment..."

"Mike," still holding onto her hand, he lifted the other to finger the steel dogtags dangling in the middle of his sweating, thickly muscled chest. "Mike Flanagan. I'm back. You must be Heather. Nan's told me all about you."

Heather wanted to sink into the floor with humiliation; *how* had she not realized who he had to be? "She told me about you, too," she stuttered. "Only she didn't mention that you were six foot four and built like a battle tank; somehow in her stories you always had a dirty face and skinned knees."

Mike threw his head back and roared with laughter. "Pretty sure I'm still eight in Nan's head," he said with a broad smile when he stopped laughing. "Bless her."

"She's been very kind to me..." Mrs Flanagan had let Heather take the apartment without references and with only two weeks' deposit, getting her out of the hell her previous relationship had turned into.

"She thinks the world of you," Mike said quietly.

"Only because I know ASL, I think," Heather admitted. "My stepmother was deaf, so I learned as a kid. I'd forgotten some, but talking with your grandmother has helped."

Mike nodded slowly, his eyes scanning subtly up and down Heather's body. His grandmother hadn't exactly been accurate with the physical description; she'd described Heather as 'just a bit of a thing, looks like the wind could blow her away', but then all the Flanagans were big, tall folks. Heather wasn't tiny, but she was probably a little below average height, maybe five foot three at his best guess. She had some serious curves too, shown off nicely by the sweat-damp T-shirt that was all she was wearing. He tried, and failed, to keep his eyes from lingering on her breasts, on the plump nipples shoving against the thin fabric.

Spotting the direction of his gaze, Heather backpedaled. "Well, I, yeah. Just came out because I thought you were delivering a parcel or something. But since you're supposed to be here, it's all good! Nice to meet you! Bye!"

Her apartment door slammed in Mike's face and he groaned, mentally kicking himself for being a lecherous idiot.

I've scared her off already. Nan's gonna kill me...

Heather leaned back against the closed door, breath coming fast, heart pounding as if she'd just run a race. The way Mike had looked at her hadn't frightened her; no, it had aroused her in a way she hadn't felt in far, far too long.

"Get over yourself," she tried to tell herself sternly, but failed. Hurrying into the bathroom, she turned the faucet on to splash cold water on her face and groaned at what she saw in the mirror. That was what Mike had seen, that flushed, sweating woman, long brown curls a tangled mess around her shoulders, eyes wide with lust, her lips red from where she'd bitten at them in frustration during her piano practice.

There was only one thing for it. Turning the faucet off, she moved over to the shower instead and turned it on full cold.

She felt a little better after the shower, although the remembered heat in Mike's eyes as he looked at her breasts had her feeling warm again almost immediately. Drying off, she caught a glimpse of herself in the mirror, paused to look properly. She did have good breasts, high and full, raspberry nipples even harder now after the insult of the chill water. Reaching up, Heather thumbed her nipples lightly, gasped at the sensation.

Gliding a hand down over her stomach, she reached between her legs, knowing already what she'd find there; welling, slick heat the cold shower had done nothing to dispel.

A knock at her apartment door made her gasp and clutch for her just-discarded towel;

wrapping it tightly around her, she called "Who is it?"

"Mike Flanagan. I'm going to the grocery store, just wondered if you want anything?"

Yes, but you can't buy it at the grocery store. "No, thanks," Heather called instead, and a moment later heard the building's front door slam.

Well. Apparently my libido really is still alive and well.

In which case, she might as well take the opportunity to try and put some of the passion back into her music, since she wasn't going to be getting any of the *other* kind of satisfaction. Grabbing a sundress from her closet, she pulled it on over still-damp skin and headed back to the piano with renewed purpose.

Lost in her music, in the euphoric transcendence that came with finally playing how she wanted to play, Heather didn't hear the increasingly frantic knocking on her door. She was unaware of anything outside the notes cascading from her fingers until a pair of strong hands landed on her shoulders, making her scream and almost fall off the piano bench with fright.

"Heather! It's me, Mike Flanagan. You're all right..." he let go of her shoulders after steadying her, took a couple of steps back with his hands raised unthreateningly. "I'm sorry I startled you."

"What the hell are you doing in here?" she gasped, hand over her pounding heart.

"Heather, it's *midnight*."

"Oh my God, I'm so sorry, you were probably trying to sleep..."

"No," he shook his head. "I was enjoying the amazing classical concert, actually, until I realized that you've been playing without a break for about *seven hours*."

"Oh." Now that she thought about it, she did feel tired, her hands and arms aching. Flexing her fingers, she offered him a smile. "Yeah, I can get a bit lost in the music. I did have a couple of short breaks..." she'd had a bottle of water, lit some tea-light candles on the piano. More light than that was unnecessary since she was playing from memory anyway, didn't need the light to read music by. "How did you get in?" she suddenly thought to ask.

"You didn't lock your door," Mike said dryly. "Which is a deeply unsafe habit, even though the front door is quite secure. I was about to go upstairs to ask Nan for your spare key when I thought to try the handle."

Heather screwed her eyes shut with embarrassment. "I was distracted, earlier."

"Yeah?" His voice was dark with amusement. "After you just met me, was that?"

He knew very well that she hadn't been anywhere since then; she'd have already been practicing by the time he got back from the grocery store. Heather took a deep breath and opened her eyes again.

"I don't often meet strange half-naked men in my hallway."

Mike laughed, that full, genuine laugh she'd heard earlier. "I should hope not! Well, we're not strangers now, are we?"

"You're still half-naked, though," her treacherous tongue pointed out, making Heather want to scream at herself in frustration.

"I'm willing to bet I've got just as many items of clothing on as you," Mike challenged wickedly, eyes raking over her bare legs beneath her sundress, sliding up to her breasts pushing against the thin fabric. "If not more."

If he's wearing underwear under those denim shorts, he'll be right, Heather realized unwillingly. "It's hot," she claimed.

"Sure is," Mike's gaze settled on her mouth. "Even though I fixed your AC, since Nan told me it had developed a fault."

It really was fixed, she realized with a sudden shock, the room felt cool for the first time in days. "Oh - thank you!"

"You're welcome." He was still looking at her mouth. Heather licked her lips uncertainly, and Mike took a small step forward, one big hand lifting to brush a stray strand of hair away from her cheek. "Can't have you overheating," his voice was low and sensuous. "Even though every time I look at you I think I'm about to spontaneously combust."

Her cheeks warmed and she cast her eyes down shyly; although that was a mistake because it made her look straight at his groin, where she could see the evidence inside his shorts that he was most definitely aroused.

Mike groaned her name and Heather looked back up at him; he was standing closer now, the look on his face unmistakably one of desire. One hand curled around under her jaw gently, his thumb brushing lightly over her lips as he gazed down at her, his eyes dark with lust.

"You got a real pretty mouth," he said hoarsely. "Makes me think about what your lips would look like wrapped around my cock."

An imp of mischief seized her; she gave him what she hoped was a seductive smile and said "Would you like to see?"

"*Fuck*, yes."

Her slender, clever fingers reached for his waistband, worked the button and zipper. He was wearing boxers beneath; Heather smiled again as she pushed them down along with his shorts. "Well, lookit that. You *are* wearing one more item of clothing than me."

"Tease," Mike said hoarsely, his hand sliding into her hair as she leaned forward, stroking through the long curly tresses, though he didn't pull, allowing her to take her time.

His member strained towards her, thick and long as she wrapped her hand around him, a gleaming pearl at the tip tempting her to lick it off before she sucked him slowly into her mouth, hollowing her cheeks, her tongue dragging slowly over the underside.

"Oh damn, yeah, that's it, sweetheart," his voice was low and rasping, his fingers tightening in her hair, tugging her forward. He wasn't rough, though, and Heather wasn't at all unwilling. Breathing through her nose she opened her throat - and *hummed* around him, deliberately making her throat vibrate around the sensitive, swollen head of his cock.

"Jesus Mary and Joseph!" Mike swore loudly. "*Fuck*, you're good, oh yeah, take it, sweetheart, take all of it."

She couldn't, she literally couldn't. He was too big; as his hips rocked, thrusting his engorged cock deep into her mouth, involuntary tears sprang to Heather's eyes and she gagged.

To her surprise, Mike pulled back immediately, dropping to a crouch in front of her so that he was at her eye level. "Fuck, I'm sorry, Heather, are you okay?"

Swiping a hand over her eyes quickly, she nodded. "Of course! I just choked a bit - you're big!"

His grin was more than a little smug, though he shrugged sheepishly. "Lost my head a bit, your mouth feels too fucking good." His finger traced slowly over her bottom lip. "Such a *pretty* mouth."

Wanting him to kiss her, Heather leaned forward, and Mike obliged, his arms going around her to hold her close to him, pulling her spread knees on either side of his body as he knelt down and drew her into his lap. She moaned against his mouth as she felt his cock rubbing at her pussy through the thin cotton of the sundress that was all that separated them.

"You want it, do ya?" Mike released her lips to kiss down her neck, his hands dropping to the hem of her sundress, lifting it up. "Want a good fucking? You look so fucking gorgeous at that piano, I want to bend you over it and fuck you senseless."

Heather moaned, her own hands busy exploring his muscled torso. There didn't seem to be an ounce of fat on him, he was all smooth, hard planes, a fine mat of hair on his chest chafing against her skin and making her shudder.

"But first, I want to taste you," and Mike was suddenly lifting her, easily moving her weight. Startled, Heather clutched at him as he stood them both up and then let go of her, walking around the piano to close the lid. "Come here, sweetheart," he beckoned to her, grinning wickedly. "Ever been debauched on your own piano before?"

A little shocked, she shook her head even as she went willingly to stand beside him. Strong hands closed on her waist and Mike lifted her easily to sit on the smooth wooden surface, pushing her skirt up to her waist.

"Well then, it's about time you were. Lay back and put your legs over my shoulders," he ordered, leaning forward.

A quiver raced through Heather at his masterful tone, and she lay back obediently, feeling the cool, polished wood against her shoulders and the backs of her arms. Mike's strong hands curled under her thighs, lifting them to press against the heated muscles of his shoulders, just before he reached up her body and tugged the top of her sundress down to make her breasts pop free.

Heather gasped as strong fingers tweaked at her nipples, at the same time as Mike's tongue lashed for the first time against her aching clit. He made an "Mm mm" sound of pleasure before licking again, long and slow from her hole right up over her clit, then scraping his upper teeth lightly over her clit as his agile tongue pushed into her pussy, hot and wet.

"Oh God, Mike, that's so good," she whimpered, her toes curling, heels digging into his muscled back. He made another pleased sound, but his mouth was far too busy for speaking, his upper lip worrying at her clit as his tongue slurped up her juices, flicking up between her labia and making her jolt and groan, her nails squeaking on the piano's polished top as she struggled to find something to anchor herself to.

Her legs started to shake uncontrollably, heat prickling up her spine. Every time Mike plucked at her nipples it sent bolts of sensation arrowing straight down to her groin, where his hot mouth worked at her, dragging her ever upwards.

A scream of pleasure erupted from her lips as the orgasm shot through her, her thigh muscles tightening so her butt lifted in the air, her head tossing from side to side, hair thrashing on the piano's lid. Mike didn't let up, though, his fingers on her nipples tightening and tugging almost painfully, his mouth fastening on her clit and suckling eagerly.

"Please," Heather sobbed, not at all sure what she was begging for. "Oh *please*." Her climax seemed to be going on and on, long-unused muscles inside her rippling as she clenched on nothing.

"Mm," Mike finally lifted his face from her, let go of her breasts and straightened up, wiping at his chin. Looking down at Heather lying debauched and trembling on the piano, he smiled, his eyes gleaming with hunger. "Look at you, you're fuckin' glorious. I'm gonna fuck you till you're screaming my name, sweet Heather."

She was pretty sure that wouldn't take much effort at all as she lay there panting, trying to get her breath back, her whole body tingling with pleasure.

Mike moved to lean over Heather, placing his hands on either side of her limp body and smiling down at her. "You okay?"

"Oh jeez, much better than just okay," she panted out. "Spectacular."

He laughed, looking pleased. "Glad to know I haven't lost my touch. Up you come." A strong hand slid under her shoulder, lifted her. She sighed and reached to put her arms around his neck, sliding down against his hard body as he lifted her down from the piano lid.

"I will never be able to look at my piano the same way, that's for sure," Heather said with a small laugh.

"I ain't finished with you and this piano yet," Mike replied with another of those wicked grins. "Let's have this off you, though," and before she could protest, he'd grasped the hem of her sundress and pulled it up, forcing her to lift her arms so he could pull it off over her head.

She lifted her hands shyly to cover her breasts, knowing she was being silly even as she did it; he'd already had his hands all over them. Mike chuckled and shook his head at her even as he discarded the dress onto the floor.

"It's a crime to hide those gorgeous boobs. They were nearly the first thing I noticed about you this afternoon, your nipples shoved up against your T-shirt. I wanted to throw that box on the floor and fuck you up against the door right then and there."

Embarrassed, Heather ducked her head as Mike gently took hold of her wrists and drew her hands down. "You're stunning," he told her quietly, "and I feel damn lucky to be here, right now."

"Oh, hush," she muttered, making him chuckle again.

"Kiss me and I'll be quiet," he enticed.

That made her laugh, but she reached up to put her arms around his neck. He had to stoop down for her, of course; the man was ridiculously tall. She felt tiny and fragile next to his muscled height. Big hands glided down her back, cupped her buttocks and lifted, so she was standing on tiptoe, his rock-hard arousal rubbing against her soft stomach.

"Fucking glorious ass, too," Mike muttered, abandoning her mouth to kiss down her neck, nipping lightly at the soft skin below her ear. "Come here and turn around, gorgeous."

Heather looked blankly at the keyboard as he guided her to stand in front of it, pushing the piano stool back with his foot. "You want me to play?"

"If you think you can while I'm fucking you senseless, sure," Mike bent his head to nibble on her shoulder, suckling slowly, leaving a blooming bruise that made Heather sway back against him with a needy moan.

"N-no, I don't think I could do that," she gasped.

"Then you better close the lid on those keys, because otherwise this could get noisy." His hands were back on her breasts, molding them into his big palms, squeezing her nipples between his fingertips. She could feel his cock rubbing between the cheeks of her ass.

Heather's hands shook as she closed the keyboard lid, leaned forward and placed her hands on top of it. "Like this?" she cast a coy look back at Mike over her shoulder.

"Hell, yeah," he breathed, gazing at her ass, at the soft curve of her spine as she deliberately arched her back, thrusting her ass out towards him. "Fuck, Heather, I'm gonna fuck you so good."

She moaned as his big hands caressed slowly over her ass, tracing downwards to tease at her inner thighs, making her move her feet a little further apart. Two long fingers pressed forward to push inside her, moving torturously slowly. Heather moaned again, trying to shove herself back hard on his fingers.

"Please, Mike, I really need it, I want that big cock in me. I want you to fuck me *hard*."

"Yeah?" He chuckled roughly, twisting his fingers inside her before delivering a light smack to her ass with his free hand. "Greedy little thing, aintcha, sweetheart?"

She yelped when he spanked her, going up on her toes. "Yes, yes, I'm so greedy. You should punish me. Definitely." Her voice was thin and desperate, she knew, but she couldn't make herself care. Heat was spreading across her skin from where Mike's hand had slapped down, and she was sure she was pouring slick onto his fingers. Two fingers had become three, thrusting roughly inside her, making her sob with need and grind herself against them. "Please," she sobbed. "Please, Mike..."

"Goddammit," he grated harshly. "How the hell could any man refuse that?" His fingers slid out of her, making Heather cry out with loss, only to groan blissfully a moment later as his hands clamped down on her hips and the blunt, flared head of his cock pushed at her. Her eyes rolled back in her head as he pushed in slowly, hips rocking in slow, gentle thrusts.

"Ahhh, that feels so good," Mike grunted. "You're tight, sweetheart, so tight around me - been a while for you?"

She nodded, glad that he couldn't see her pink cheeks. One of his big hands left her hip, gathered a handful of her thick hair and pulled slowly, arching her back further as he pressed still deeper, making a low moan come from her throat.

"Right there?" Mike asked. "That where you like it, right *there*? Do you like it hard too, Heather? Fast and rough?" His rhythm was increasing as he spoke, hips snapping faster back and forth, plunging to full depth inside her before withdrawing almost completely.

"Yes!" she yelled, her voice cracking. "Give it to me *rough* Mike, oh, oh God that's so good!" His hand was a slow remorseless tug in her hair, the small pain adding to the building ecstasy inside her. The head of his cock was running right over her G-spot with every thrust, the already-sensitive flesh feeling almost bruised as he slammed against her.

A tiny part of her mind recognized that he wasn't using his full strength; with those muscles, he could probably snap her in half if he wanted to. He let go of her hip just then, curled his forearm around her stomach, bracing her so that he could thrust harder without slamming her into the piano, but she was still being jolted around like a rag doll by the force of Mike's thrusts.

He stopped after a few more thrusts, and pulled out, jarring a wail of loss from Heather. "Please, Mike!" she begged desperately.

"Gonna take care of you, don't you worry." Sitting down on the piano bench, he grabbed her by the waist, turned her around. "Sit on me. I want to see those gorgeous boobs bouncing."

He was straddling the bench sideways, his cock jutting upwards. A little awkwardly Heather put her hands on his shoulders, swung a leg across him and gasped as he pulled her firmly straight downwards.

"Oh, God..." her head tipped back as his cock filled her completely.

"Still not my name you're screaming," Mike said roughly, grasping her ass in both hands and bracing his feet on the floor to jerk his hips up hard.

She spared a moment to think that it was a very good thing his grandmother was deaf, before the amazing sensations she was getting from Mike's thorough fucking drove every thought right out of her head. Screaming his name loudly, clawing at his shoulders, she shuddered through a second climax, her body clenching hard around him.

Mike stilled and groaned, holding Heather close, closing his eyes with pleasure as sleek internal muscles sucked on his cock. "Fuck, sweetheart, that's even better than your beautiful mouth," he pressed kisses against her sweating shoulder as she shivered against him.

Heather could only moan, clinging to him desperately. "So good," she whimpered at last. "Feels so full."

"You *are* full, sweetheart, stuffed full of my cock. You like that, don't you?" he tangled a hand in her hair again, pulling lightly to arch her back, his other hand coming up to caress her breasts, pluck at one aching nipple.

"Yes," she panted, rolling her hips as his rocked back and forth. "Yes, I love having a big thick cock shoved up in me."

"Gorgeous," Mike looked down between them, to where he could see the root of his cock plunged into her cleft. "You feel amazing on me. Hot and wet and tight. How long is it since you had a good fucking like this?"

She was already flushed with arousal and exertion, but the way she cast her eyes down told Mike everything. "A while, huh? Probably why you're just as horny as I am. I just got back from a ten-month deployment."

"That's why you're bothering with me..." the self-deprecating words spilled from Heather's mouth before she could stop herself. Mike looked astonished.

"That's what you think? Fuck, no. I'm here with you because you're fucking gorgeous and I wanted you the first moment I saw you." He squeezed her nipple, rolling it between finger and thumb to make her gasp. "I wanted to be right here, like this. Fucking up into you and making you clench around me. Seeing those pretty eyes all glazed over with lust."

Mike's hips were shifting again, and he let go of her hair and put his hand back under her ass, bracing her for his thrusts. Heather clutched at his broad shoulders, lifting her legs to wrap them around his lean hips, trying to get even closer, take him still deeper.

"That's it," Mike grunted, still tugging on her nipple, his other hand squeezing on her ass hard. "That's it, Heather, you want it, don't you? You want me to fill you up with my cum. Are you gonna come again for me?"

"Yes," she moaned, "oh, please, Mike..." the shift in angle had him rubbing right over her G-spot again, so sensitive it almost hurt. "Fill me up," she begged, "I want to feel you dripping out of me, running down my thighs..."

"Yes," his voice was tight, his fingers dropping from her breast. He put his hand flat on her belly and thumbed at her throbbing, aching clit. "Come on then. Come on me, milk it outta me, I'll give you what you want but you gotta take it."

Heather had some leverage now with her feet on the piano bench behind him and his broad shoulders to hang onto; she started to push back, rocking into his thrusts. Their bodies slapped together wetly with every movement, squelching sounds coming from her pussy as Mike's cock shuttled in and out, in and out, getting faster and faster, his thumb rubbing insistently over her clit with every stroke.

"Come on," he gasped, "come on, beautiful, that's it." His hand on her ass slipped down, curving lower, under her buttock. The tip of one finger pressed firmly against her hole, well lubricated from her own juices.

Heather cried out, straining against him, as Mike's finger slowly pushed into her ass. It felt intrusive but amazing, filling her up even more. "Mike!" she screamed his name at the ceiling, throwing her head back, heard his harsh laugh. He kissed at her neck, sucking in a thick bruise, the pain making her feel like she was so close to tipping over the edge, *so* close with his thumb skidding over her clit, his finger in her ass.

The single finger suddenly became two, pushing in firmly, and Heather lost herself, spasming and shrieking with ecstasy, her whole body clenching around Mike. He groaned her name roughly, hips jolting upwards once more, heat flooding inside her as his cock spurted thick ribbons of cum deep inside her welcoming heat.

Barely able to breathe, still seeing stars, Heather collapsed against Mike, resting her forehead on his shoulder. He shifted to free his hands and then put both his arms around her, stroking her back soothingly.

"You okay, sweetheart?"

"Unh," she made an incoherently happy noise against his shoulder, making him chuckle quietly.

"I'll take that as a yes."

They stayed close for a few moments, and then Heather began to feel uncomfortably sticky. She shifted a little. Mike hummed against her neck.

"You want to get off, huh?"

"I already did," she quipped lightly, making him chuckle deeply. His cock twitched inside her, making her gasp.

"Mm," Mike nuzzled her neck. "Okay," he said finally on a sigh, putting both hands under Heather's ass. "In a minute."

Heather squawked and clutched onto him as he stood straight up, lifting her easily, and moved off the piano bench before carrying her into her bedroom. It was pretty dark in here without the light from the candles but Mike seemed to have no trouble seeing; he carried her straight to the bed before finally lifting her off his cock and laying her down.

He was handling her like she weighed nothing, which she most certainly didn't, but it was a really nice feeling. Feeling a little shy lying naked and thoroughly debauched in front of him, Heather felt for the coverlet and pulled it over her. Mike laughed, a low, husky sound which trembled through her still-quivering core, and reached to switch on the lamp by the bed.

"No need to cover up now, sweetheart. I've seen it all, and boy is it a beautiful sight."

"Not beautiful," she mumbled into the edge of the coverlet.

"Yes. You are." His tone left no room for argument, as he sat down on the edge of the bed, took her face between both big hands and leaned in to kiss her soundly. "Beauty is in the eye of the beholder, which is me, right? And in my eyes you are very, very fucking beautiful." Gently he plucked the coverlet from her hands, drew it down over her body. "Far, far too beautiful to pull this over you when you're all hot and bothered. You'll overheat."

"Too late," Heather admitted. Her whole body was quite flushed, she was sure, as Mike's eyes scanned lasciviously up and down her naked form.

"Yeah, you got me pretty heated as well," he murmured, reaching to trace his fingers in a slow circle around one breast. Her nipple peaked again as he spiraled his fingertips up to it, and he smiled and leaned down to kiss at it lightly. Heather had to bite down on another moan as his hot tongue swirled wetly around the sensitive peak.

"Don't be quiet," Mike urged, reaching to tweak her other nipple. "You make real pretty noises. Let me hear them, there's nobody else gonna hear you."

Knowing he spoke the truth, she unclenched her teeth and tried to relax into his ministrations; within a few minutes he had her moaning and gasping, crying out with abandon once more as he played with her breasts, sucking her nipple deep into his mouth and tonguing it, rolling the other in his fingertips firmly.

Mike's seed was wet and sticky between her thighs, but he didn't seem to care as his hand slid down over her stomach and parted her legs, delving once again into her heated cleft. It was almost too much for Heather's sensitized body; she shuddered and panted his name, her fingers clawing at the sheets beneath her as he scissored callused fingertips gently around her clit.

"This okay?" he asked, a low rasp entering his voice again, and as he straightened up she saw that his other hand was wrapped around his thick member, jacking it steadily back to full arousal. "Because seeing you lying here like this, I want to fuck you again."

"Yes," she panted, "just... gentle, this time? Please?"

"Been a bit rough on you, have I?" One corner of his mouth twisted up in a smile. "Sorry about that. I'm very turned on."

"I see that," she murmured, wide-eyed at the sheer speed with which he was recuperating. "Been a while for you too, has it?"

"A barracks in Afghanistan isn't exactly the best place to meet girls," Mike said with such a rueful grin that she had to laugh.

"I'm not going to complain since I'm getting the benefits of your being sex-deprived. Aah," she had to shut her eyes as his thick fingers burrowed deep into her soaked pussy again, thumb swiping quick circles over her swollen, sensitized clit.

"As long as you're having a good time, beautiful." He slipped his hand out of her and shifted around to kneel between her legs, hooked a hand under one knee to lift it.

"A really good time," Heather gasped as his blunt tip nudged at her again. She lifted her other leg to hook it around his hips, greedily pulling him closer, drawing him in. Mike grunted, his eyes hooding with lust as he stared down at her.

"Grab your breasts for me," he told her, "squeeze those nipples, I can tell how much you like having them played with."

She did adore having her breasts touched. Cupping her hands under them and lifting them as though offering them up to him, she flicked the tips of her index fingers lightly over the swollen nipples, sighing with pleasure as the sensations shivered through her.

"Oh, too pretty," Mike groaned, bowing his back so that he could bend his head, scrape his tongue over one nipple even as his thick erection pushed slowly into Heather. "So fucking hot, sweetheart, feels so good inside you."

"Yes," she gasped breathlessly as he drove remorselessly in to the hilt, filling her completely. "Yes. Oh, Mike, that's it..." he'd worked a hand between them, rubbing his thumb over her clit again, almost sending Heather into orbit. He bit down lightly on her nipple, making her shudder and reach up, running her fingers over his short-shaven hair, scraping her nails lightly down the back of his neck.

"Mmm," Mike's hips rocked slowly, his lips let go of her nipple and his tongue licked a long messy stripe up her neck before he sought her mouth with his again. "Damn, you taste good," he muttered against her lips.

Heather hummed back against his mouth with pleasure, making him smile. He straightened up off her, sitting back on his heels, pulling her bottom up into his lap easily. Looking down at their joined bodies, he kept slowly circling her clit with the very tip of his thumb.

"Aaahh," that felt even better. Heather flung her arms up over her head, grabbing onto the headboard and arching her back, trying to push back into Mike's thrusts. She'd entirely forgotten that she'd asked him to be gentle; now she just wanted him to fuck her roughly again, hard and fast to satisfy the craving he'd awakened in her. "Do it," she gasped, "*fuck* me, Mike, give it to me!"

He groaned with pleasure, strong fingers digging into her ass as he held her tightly. His thumb never ceased its movements over her clit as he accelerated his thrusts, driving deep again and again, their bodies slapping wetly together repeatedly as his thick cock slammed in and out of her dripping pussy.

Heather was completely unaware how much noise she was making; joyous screams of pleasure echoing from the walls making Mike grin ferally down at her. His dog tags swung above her bouncing breasts, her dark hair thrashed on the pillow as she flung her head from side to side, her eyes closed as she gave herself over to the sensations coursing through her.

"Come on, Heather," Mike rasped. "Come on, sweetheart, once more, you can do it. Milk it outta me, take it all."

She couldn't get out a coherent word, only desperate cries of ecstasy as he slammed into her with all his considerable strength. Sweat slicked both their straining bodies despite the air-conditioned room, panting breaths and pounding hearts in perfect sync as they took pleasure in each other's willing, needy bodies.

"Aww, fuck, fuck," Mike groaned as he felt his balls pull up tight to his body. Heather was just too much, too giving, too glorious in her abandon. "Fuck, baby..."

"Please," she sobbed, and he found from somewhere the strength to grit his teeth and hold on for just a few thrusts more, until he felt her suddenly convulse around him, her leg muscles tightening as her heels dug into his ass, strong internal muscles sucking at him. He shouted wordlessly as the climax ripped through him, thick pulses of cum jetting up his cock to spurt inside Heather's soaking, clutching pussy as she rode out her own release with low, throaty screams of ecstasy ringing in his ears.

"Fu-uck," Mike's arms were shaking as he braced them on either side of Heather's body, holding himself up from collapsing onto her. "Shit. Fuck. Holy fucking hell."

Heather chuckled breathlessly. "Watch your language, soldier."

"Hah," he leaned down to kiss her briefly, but they were both too out of breath to maintain the kiss for long. "Sorry, beautiful. Barracks language."

"It's okay," her slender, long-fingered hands came up, caressed lightly over his shoulders. "I was teasing. It's quite flattering, that I made you want to curse like that."

"Sweetheart, you make me want to do a whole lot of things." Leaning down onto one elbow, mindful that his heavy weight could crush her, he smoothed his fingers lightly over her tangled hair, touched her cheek lightly. "You have since the moment I saw you earlier, wearing that thin little shirt that I could see your nipples through, and flashing me that pretty pussy as you fell on your rump."

"I *what*?" her eyes flew wide.

"The saying goes '*you had me at hello*', but you had me hooked well before that, sweetheart." He was laughing at her with his eyes, but there was nothing unkind about it.

"Oh my God, I made an even bigger fool of myself than I realized!" Thinking back, Heather groaned with mortification. The way she'd landed with her legs spread probably had given him a perfect view that she hadn't been wearing any panties.

Mike grinned and kissed her again. "Trust me. *Foolish* is not how I thought you looked. Sexy, stunning, a sight for sore eyes. The kind of girl a guy dreams about finding out is his next door neighbor. *That's* what I thought."

She was too red from exertion to blush any deeper, but she cast her eyes down and smiled shyly. "I didn't exactly expect to find a gorgeous, muscular soldier moving in next door, either."

"Seems like we both lucked out." Mike didn't really feel inclined to move, but his weight had to be pressing down on Heather uncomfortably, and she was very flushed, sweating and over-heated from their exertion. Slowly, carefully, he eased back, rolled to his side, laying his hand on her stomach gently.

"I need the bathroom," Heather mumbled uncomfortably, and Mike sighed. He'd have to get up to let her out, and it was hardly an opportune moment to ask if he could stay the night - what was left of it, anyway - as she clutched a sheet to her and fled. Padding back out to the piano, he picked up his shorts and tugged them back on, resigned to returning to his own bed alone.

"You're going?" Heather's voice said softly, and he looked around to see her standing in the doorway to the bedroom, the sheet still draped around her, the lamplight behind her silhouetting her shapely figure.

Heather bit her lip disappointedly as she saw Mike pulling his clothes on. She hadn't really expected roses and happily-ever-afters, but that he wasn't even going to stay the night - that hurt a little bit. The words spurted from her mouth before she could stop herself.

"You're going?"

You idiot, Heather, you just made yourself sound like the dumbest, clingiest woman ever...

She blinked with surprise as Mike turned back towards her and came striding over, his long-limbed, loose stride covering the distance between them quickly. Warm hands settled on her shoulders, his deep brown eyes searched hers.

"I'd love to stay, but you should really get some sleep, and that bed's on the small side."

That was actually quite true, she realized, looking over her shoulder at her standard double bed and then back at Mike's tall, broad frame. He'd have to lie diagonally across it to get his whole body on the bed, or his feet would dangle uncomfortably off the end. "Oh." It was a perfectly valid reason, but she still felt irrationally disappointed.

"Of course," Mike placed two fingers under her chin, tipped it up gently and leaned down to kiss her lingeringly again, "you could always come over to my place."

"Wh-what?" He'd turned her brain to mush yet again with that kiss.

"My place. I'm not exactly fully moved in yet, but the bed's a California King and I haven't even slept on the sheets yet," he enticed. "Why don't you come on over and help me break it in? We might even get some sleep. Eventually."

Heather had to laugh, but she also let him take her hand and lead her towards the door and across the hallway into his apartment. She should have been far too exhausted to even think about more sex, but as Mike unwound the sheet from around her and drew her gently down onto the giant-sized, freshly made bed, she opened her arms to him with an inviting smile.

"Well, hello there, soldier."

"Nice to meet ya, neighbor," he replied with a hungry grin. "How do you do?"

~ *The End* ~

CAITLYN LYNCH

ABOUT THE AUTHOR

Caitlyn Lynch is an Australian author who loves writing about sexy people finding their happily ever after together!

You can connect with her on her website at

www.caitlynlynch.com

CAITLYN LYNCH

www.ingramcontent.com/pod-product-compliance
Lightning Source LLC
Chambersburg PA
CBHW020619120726
47905CB00003B/853